AN ALGERIAN HERO

CARLOS ESTRADA

Published in the United States by Carlos Estrada.

ISBN: 979-8-218-26874-9
E-book ISBN: 979-8-218-32728-6

Printed in the United States of America.

Book design by Vivien Reis

ALGIERS, 1961

I

Dark, gray skies hovered above the city of Algiers during the early morning hour on the fourth day of January, 1961. Residents out and about on the city streets were bundled up in comfy winter coats and jackets, amidst the chilly air. For Karim Brahimi though, a penniless teenager, sporting a long-sleeved white shirt under a thin navy blue cardigan and the usual slacks, he shivered on occasion, ill-equipped to deal with the cold conditions. A cluster of palm trees stood in front of the Hôtel de la Régence and he took temporary refuge under one to minimize getting wet as much as possible as the drizzle of rain fell. After some wait, Karim spotted the trolley bus approaching, which pulled up close to the Duc d'Orléans statue and adjacent to the Mosque of the Fisherman's Wharf. He hurried across the street to the main square, La Place du Gouvernement, all but deserted given the current weather conditions, save for those standing at the curb to board the trolley bus. Out in the distance, one could see the calm waters that was the Bay of Algiers.

Karim boarded the trolley bus, surprised to find that it was packed with passengers. A police officer was on hand, and right away he stopped Karim and performed *la fouille*, the up-and-down body search to ensure that he was not carrying anything lethal in his possession, even searching the messenger bag, which carried his books, strapped over his shoulder. Such a search of an Algerian was all the more encouraged due to the recent Muslim riots that shook the city only weeks earlier. As the trolley bus continued in its course, Karim sensed the eyes focusing in on him, from a number of those of European descent. A stare that, for all intents and purposes, elicited a *what are you doing here?* type of look. He guessed that he was one of no more than a few Algerians on board.

He exited the trolley bus and headed to Les Tailleurs du Monde, a tailor shop located on the winding Rue Rovigo, to pick up his blue blazer coat that was a part of his school uniform—one that was overdue for a much-needed alteration. Entering the shop, Karim waited his turn. A well-dressed Frenchman who seemed to be in no rush whatsoever, stood in front of the counter interacting with the woman behind it, Amandine, the owner of the establishment. A newspaper rested at the far end of the counter. Karim moved to the paper, finding it convenient to begin scanning through it as a means to help pass the time. Printed at the top in big, bold letters enclosed in a red rectangle: *EL MOUDJAHID*. Indeed, this was the newspaper of the FLN, *Front de Libération Nationale*, Algeria's revolutionary movement. The front page featured a woman brandishing an Algerian flag during a public demonstration. Below it, the headline read: "*Le drapeau algérien flotte à Alger.*" The Algerian flag flies in Algiers. In scanning through the fine print and images in the subsequent pages, he came upon an image–a photo of an ALN soldier, fighting in the FLN's army, clutching an automatic rifle, perhaps stationed in some rural region far from the capital city. In another article, a call to all fellow Algerians to join in the fight to free themselves from the European colonizer.

As Karim turned the page, another patron entered the shop. A quick turn over the shoulder, glancing at the man for a second, no more than two, and Karim shifted his focus back to the paper. The patron who was being tended to finally finished and Karim, knowing he didn't want the next patron to cut in front of him, called out to the owner Amandine to retrieve his blazer coat for pickup, handing her the receipt. He returned to the far end of the counter, resuming his read of the paper, now intrigued by the content. Yet, Karim now realized that time was of the essence and he needed to hurry and head to school. Flipping to the next page, the other lone patron in the shop hovered over his shoulder, standing behind him. "Find something intriguing?" the man asked, stocky, short buzz haircut, a rough five o'clock shadow gracing his face.

Karim was startled by the tall figure looming over him, retreating a couple of footsteps. "You scared me."

"My apologies. Didn't mean to."

"Well, I do find articles about war intriguing, though maybe not for the reasons that one might think. This is quite interesting material here," Karim said, shifting his eyes to the paper.

"That's not what I meant exactly."

Amandine called out for Karim. "Your blazer coat is ready."

Karim quickly paid the bill and retrieved his blazer coat. The patron approached him, eager to prolong the dialogue. "Hey listen. Why don't we–"

Karim interrupted. "I'm sorry, I don't mean to be rude and cut you off, but I'm running late and need to get to school."

"I won't take much more of your time. Can we just chat outside for a couple of minutes?"

Karim shrugged his shoulders and gave in. "Sure, just make it quick."

Both men stepped outside into the chilly morning breeze circulating around them and the stranger continued, "I have to ask, where did you get that newspaper from? Is it yours?"

"It's not mine. It was just sitting there on the counter."

"Do you know that *El Moudjahid* is a publication in exile? Copies aren't even printed in Algeria. Copies of the paper have to be smuggled into Algeria from Tunisia."

"Really?" Karim replied, stunned. "Don't know anything about it."

"Which is why I asked where the copy came from. I wondered how you got your hands on it."

"I see. But what does all this have to do with me?"

"Anyhow, I noticed what you were reading and would like to discuss a proposal with you, in a setting where we'll have more privacy. Can we meet this weekend and discuss it in detail? Say Saturday?"

"Saturday is fine, I suppose. It's my day off from school. What kind of private setting do you have in mind?"

"El-Kettar Cemetery. Say ten in the morning?"

"That works for me."

"Excellent. I'm Sofiane, by the way," the man said, extending his hand out for a shake, which Karim reciprocated.

"Karim."

"Look forward to seeing you there."

The Algerian War had entered its seventh year. For the French, Algeria remained its crown jewel in all of colonial Africa, even more so after its colonies Morocco and Tunisia gained their independence just a few years earlier. Karim, a seventeen-year-old high school student, was born and raised in the Casbah of Algiers. He'd lived in Algiers most of his life, save for a few years living in a rural village in Kabylia. Lean built and tall, at least for his age, Karim featured bushy eyebrows and short, curly black hair. His father, Amir, was killed in an ambush, likely a result of a reprisal, an attack that Karim witnessed with his very own eyes; a memory that still haunted him to this day. The oldest of four children, he lived poor his entire life.

Karim attended the prestigious Lycée Bugeaud. A result of a fluke, perhaps, as trouble followed Karim seemingly everywhere he went in life. Involved in mischief and petty theft, he often stole loaves of bread from local bakeries in order to feed himself and his family, a criminal act that landed him in juvenile prison for over a year. Karim justi-fied his past thefts and mischiefs as not being in the wrong, since, after all, as he viewed it, he was disadvantaged in society and *the settlers who were more well-off could bear the loss as they were the oppressors.*

The vagueness from Sofiane was all the more reason for Karim to meet up with him. It more or less toyed with the mind of a teenager who lacked the ability, or experience, to discern what was right from wrong; what would keep him on the right track or lead him astray. As Karim began on foot, on his way to El-Kettar Cemetery that Saturday morning, the only solid idea he had in mind as to Sofiane's purpose for the meeting was that it had to have something to do with the FLN. He had nothing to lose by meeting up with him.

Karim arrived early at the cemetery, situated on a steep hill. A cemetery designated for Muslims, as the tombstones of dead Europeans lay in other burial grounds in the city. He followed a dirt walkway in ascending the hill, with some tombstones surrounded by dirt, while for many others, grass and plants in contrast. With no specific meeting spot within the cemetery, Karim strolled along the walkway. Sofiane was nowhere in sight. To pass the time, Karim meandered past one grave after another, of tombstones bearing names of Algerians who had died prior to the start of the conflict. He then took refuge under a tree. Up to that point, Karim had seen only two visitors at the cemetery.

He kept his eyes on the lookout, scanning the landscape for Sofiane. Within minutes, a figure emerged from the far end of the walkway. Indeed it was him.

"Pleased to see you here. I was worried that you'd have second thoughts about showing up," Sofiane said, eager to give Karim a firm handshake.

"I'm a man of my word," Karim replied.

"This year will bring many blessings to our people, I can see it."

Cautiously optimistic, Karim uttered, "Well yes, of course. I'm hopeful of it. But not if more and more Algerians are being killed."

"That's why we need to create our own destiny and act on it. Otherwise, we will always be subservient to the colonizer."

Karim shook his head. "And it's been so long."

"What I'm about to reveal to you, please keep it confidential."

"Sure."

"I am the Minister of Foreign Affairs for the FLN."

Beyond hearing that very acronym, the mystery status of Sofiane now revealed itself, yet one that was somewhat greater than what Karim first suspected. "Wow. You must be a man of tremendous influence within, I'll say."

"I'm up at the top of the hierarchy, the totem pole, as others may say."

Karim met Sofiane's eyes. "So what cause led you to invite me here?"

"Recruitment," Sofiane answered bluntly.

"What, are you referring to me?" Karim replied, dumbfounded.

Sofiane stretched his hand out to the walkway, motioning Karim to join him in proceeding down the path. Both men began the stroll and Sofiane continued, "Not to boast in any way, but I have this keen sense of spotting gifted individuals. And that's what I saw in you when I met you the other day...So, my request is this: I'd like for you to join the FLN."

Karim's eyes widened. *Did I hear that correctly?*, he wondered. "I'm just a student," he answered.

"And after you finish your studies, what good will that do for you when the economic and political rights are still stacked against your favor?" Sofiane replied, a direct rebuttal.

Karim dipped his head. "I know. I can't deny that." He then looked up, and in the direction of Sofiane. "First of all, before we get ahead of ourselves, what does all of this entail? What would I be getting myself involved in?"

"I'll be engaging in assignments abroad, some being clandestine in nature. So, we need someone who can carry out missions here in Algiers, and, at times, the mountainous regions, even the Mitidja. But mainly in Algiers."

"But what exactly? What missions, or assignments are you referring to?" Karim pressed, still non-committal.

"The movement of arms, money, striking enemy targets, to name a few."

"But I'm just a student," Karim repeated, "and a poor one at that. For me to join, it will need to be worthwhile–I'll need to be compensated, in some way."

"Rest assured, you'll be adequately remunerated and well fed."

Karim was not entirely swayed, yet to be won over. "Have others filled this role before?"

"Yes, in fact."

"And what was the result?"

"I've had many quit or terminated because they weren't a good fit, didn't follow orders or had ulterior motives. Basically, I want to find out if you're up for the job."

"This is a lot for me to take in, you know."

"I know you're up to the task."

A light drizzle kicked in. "Let's head over to my car," Sofiane said.

They made it to Sofiane's vehicle, a black Mercedes Benz 170 S, parked on a street adjacent to the cemetery. He opened the rear door and reached for a wool coat, handing it to Karim. "This is for you," he said, to which Karim was ever grateful for it.

Sofiane invited Karim to join him for an early lunch, at a place that he raved about, and was met with a quick agreement. Inside the car, the two engaged in small talk, and headed just down the street, no more than a few-minutes' drive. They arrived at a small, hole-in-the-wall restaurant. Both men were seated right away by a man who appeared to be well acquainted with Sofiane, and ordered promptly.

"So, you prefer a young man in his late teens rather than a man who is, say, in his thirties or so, for the job, right?" Karim asked.

"I do, and the reasons are rather obvious: More vigor, youthful energy, easier for me to mold into the right partner," Sofiane replied. "*And mold into the right partner*," he stressed, a verbal underline, "something I cannot emphasize enough."

"Makes a lot of sense."

"Formal education also helps. It's not a deal-breaker, but a huge plus, I should say."

"Only high school for me."

"That's adequate enough. Many within the ranks don't even have that."

"How can that be?"

Sofiane shrugged his shoulders. "Eh, favoritism, nepotism, the tribe that you descend from, among other things."

The meal arrived. A large, hearty *shakshuka*–a spicy tomato dish with poached eggs–served in an ornate silver pan with double handles, and alongside loaves of *kesra*–Algerian bread. The aroma from the *shakshuka* was tantalizing to say the least. Karim was starving. "Couldn't have come at a better time," he said.

"Dig in, and eat as much as you wish," Sofiane replied.

A young man who always had little to eat, Karim tore off a piece of bread and dunked it into the moist egg yolk, then scooped up a spoonful of tomato sauce, followed by a ravenous bite. Sofiane excused himself to head outside and smoke a cigarette. By the time he returned, the dish was all gone. The two walked out the door of the restaurant shortly after, heading back to the car.

"France is vulnerable under de Gaulle. He lacks unity behind his people. It's our moment, our opportunity to seize and reclaim our sovereignty. As long as we remain resolute, determined, *Algérie Française* will be put to rest once and for all," Sofiane said.

"What have they done for us?" Karim replied.

"They've left us powerless, and in a status as second-class citizens on our own land."

"Even a young man like me, I'm starting to see where you're going at here…"

Sofiane stood right beside him by the passenger's door and asked, "So, what do you say?"

"Count me in."

For better or for worse, Sofiane left a lasting impression on Karim. Sofiane carried himself with purpose, resolute, unyielding in what he sought, and it was enough to convince Karim to associate himself with this stranger who held tremendous influence and power within the FLN. As Sofiane said, the time was ripe for the FLN to fulfill its destiny, under leadership that refused to accept anything less than full sovereignty and independence. Being young and agile, Karim was an ideal fit, so he came to believe, to join the ranks of the FLN and to leave his mark in imposing the will and voice of Algeria's revolutionaries.

January 9. Karim was on his way to school at two-thirty in the afternoon. He skipped class that day, conferring with Sofiane for preparations of his first assignment. A partly cloudy day with rather strong winds, cars passing along the Place Jean Mermoz, situated between the high school and the Pélissier barracks. The abruptness of cars being brought to a halt due to careless teens jaywalking on the street, with little to no thought for utilizing a pedestrian crossing at a stoplight.

Arriving on campus, Karim came to a throng of students, several of whom he recognized, descending the main stair steps outside, dismissed from school for the day. To many of his classmates and the school's faculty, Karim was seen as an *évolué* due to him being educated at this *lycée* and the way he dressed–in a school uniform. He entered the hall and proceeded to the reception office to speak to the principal. First, Karim came to the secretary, Alexandra. On hearing Karim's request, she said nothing, and, pencil in hand between the thumb and index finger, gestured with the pencil in pointing in the direction behind her, motioning Karim to head straight to the principal's office. The principal, a Languedoc native in his sixties named Christophe Renaud, wasn't in much of a talking mood himself either. The explanation Karim provided for his absence from class was that of fabricating some lame story of his sister's illness. Nevertheless, the principal did not bother questioning it whatsoever.

Onward to chat with his history professor, Didier Cachot, a man who, over time, had become more of a father figure to Karim, and, in turn, one of the very few Frenchmen whom Karim held in high reverence and respect. The classroom door was wide open and, as Karim stood in front of it, Professor Cachot was wiping off the chalkboard with an eraser. He turned to his left, facing Karim.

"Karim, you were absent from class today," the professor said. "What's going on?"

Karim took several steps forward to the professor's desk. "Well, there's a good reason why I missed class."

"It's unlike you to skip class." He set down the eraser. "Have a seat," Didier said, motioning to the chair beside the desk.

"No, I'm fine."

Instead, Didier took a seat himself and reached for a pencil, as if he was about to take notes. A man in his late-forties who often wore cream-colored clothing, including shoes, he had salt-and-pepper hair that was fairly short on the sides, and long at the top, neatly combed back. Thin, clean shaven, bearing a light chestnut brown skin complexion, which had been attributed to suntanning on the French Riviera, as well as the Algerian coast. Born and raised in Algiers, he traced his family roots to the Provence region. Didier lacked in height; in fact, he was shorter than Karim, three decades his junior.

"There's something I need to tell you, and it's not an easy thing to do, I must say," Karim admitted, spinning the apple resting on top of the desk. "But I will cease attending class. I will be quitting school."

The professor was taken aback, lost in bewilderment. "I don't understand."

"It's a difficult decision to make."

"But I don't get it. I mean, you were struggling in class at the start of the school year, but the past month or so, you've been coming along quite strong. I've seen immense improvement."

"There's something greater at play here, for me."

"Like what? What could be more important than your education, your future?" Didier moved over to the door to close it, allowing for total privacy from the random student passing along the corridor who might overhear their conversation, before returning to his seat.

Karim paced himself with slow steps halfway toward the window at the other side of the classroom, contemplating how to phrase his looming admission. Above all, it was simply a matter of mustering the courage to admit it. He turned around and moved towards the desk again, facing Didier. "I will be joining the FLN."

Again, Didier found himself astounded. "*C'est pas vrai.*" It can't be. He shook his head. "For what reason? I mean, you're too young for this."

"I have a greater calling, and it's one for me to act on, and the timing is now," Karim replied. "And it's nothing personal, as you know. You've been there for me, in more ways than one."

"Well, look. As a Frenchman obviously, I'm sure I may see colonization and even the current state of affairs in Algeria differently than you do. That being said, and I know I can share this with you without any regret, I'll have you know that I'm neither pro- nor anti-FLN. Likewise, I'm neither pro- nor anti-colonialist. Consider me neutral, if you will," said Didier, twirling the pencil between his index and middle fingers. His demeanor appeared to have changed from bewilderment to cool and understanding.

"Though it won't change my stance, I appreciate hearing your position on this."

"So, I won't be seeing you here in class anymore?"

"Correct."

"Have you spoken to the principal about your decision?"

"No," Karim replied with a shake of his head. "At least not yet, anyway."

"Please do. Should you have to return; if you come to

realize that this pursuit is not what you expected or it takes a turn for the worse and you then wish to resume studies, you can possibly be considered for reinstatement by the principal by following the proper protocol. You don't need to be reminded how competitive it is to be admitted to the Lycée Bugeaud."

"And to this day, it still kind of strikes me as a miracle how I was able to get admitted to this school."

"What I am saying to you is, please think and consider the long-term picture here. Have a Plan B in case things don't work out. And it'd be best for you to notify the principal and suggest you'd be open to possibly returning as a student."

"Noted. And you make valid points for me to consider."

"And your family? Their thoughts?"

"They're not enthusiastic about it," Karim admitted. "I'd be lying if I said otherwise."

"That's an appropriate reaction. Can't say I blame them."

Karim shrugged. "But," he responded, "at the end of the day, family is family, and I know I'll always have their support."

The professor rose from his chair. "Take care of yourself out there. Stay safe, and keep in touch," he said, extending his hand for a shake.

"You'll still see me," Karim replied. "And you'll always hear from me." Karim bade goodbye and walked out of the classroom, without a tinge of regret.

Sofiane was back in town, having spent time across the border in Tunisia in meeting with a delegation from the GPRA, the Provisional Government of the Algerian Republic. In addition, a warm invitation was extended to him during his trip, which he gladly accepted, to pay a visit to a remote site in the central part of the country where firearms training and military recruiting had been taking place for fellow Algerians residing in Tunisia.

The sky was sunny, albeit mild in temperature. Sofiane's car was parked in front of a *boucherie* on Boulevard Auguste Comte in the district of Belcourt. The quarter was poor and mixed, of both Algerians and *pied-noirs*, European settlers and their descendants. Muslim women in white burkas passing along the street as were the Europeans. Sofiane stood on the sidewalk, leaning against the car, his back to the driver's door, waiting for Karim. In no time, he spotted Karim, walking just feet behind a French boy carrying a small basket of sardine tins.

"Get in the car," Sofiane said, "we've got a long drive ahead of us."

Before opening the passenger's door, Karim saw a man and a woman sitting in the backseat. He suspected that both were affiliated with or members of the FLN, which he would soon learn to be correct. The woman, named Djamila, looked to be in her late teens to early twenties, dressed–apart from the headscarf–in Western attire: khakis, a white blouse and tennis shoes. Her girlish face and blushy cheeks aroused affection in Karim. The man beside her, wearing business casual attire, middle-aged, sparse balding amidst slicked back hair and high cheekbones, was named Yassine and claimed to be "involved in the political affairs" of the FLN.

They took off in the Mercedes, heading to the outskirts of Algiers and then to the highway, leaving the city. "Where to?" Karim asked.

"To the east, away from the city," Sofiane replied,

rolling up his window just a bit. "It's something that is better explained when seeing it in person."

"Many more recruits now on board?" Karim then asked, changing the subject.

"Several, to say the least. These young men are about your age and didn't have any idea how to use a firearm. They avoided the Morice Line, moving further south to the Aurès mountains, and then penetrating into Tunisia, just as they were instructed to do."

"Kids smart enough to avoid encountering barbed wire, electric fences and land mines," Yassine interjected.

"I tried crossing it once, and never again! Thankfully, I didn't lose my life. Unfortunately, many have already. In my case, I learned from experience."

"I recall you telling me Tunisia is a haven for us insurgents," Karim said to Sofiane.

"Their government has been welcoming and accommodating to us," Sofiane replied.

"So all of these recruits are young men?"

"No, not at all. The older men, most of whom are from the *bled*, are also more of the illiterate types. Not only can they not speak French, but they even struggle with Arabic. They're more at ease in their Berber dialects though."

"My parents don't speak French either, and I don't blame them. As they say, 'Why should I have to cater to them when they've colonized our land?'" Djamila interjected.

"I still believe that the only way we're going to achieve victory is through diplomacy, not through military conflict. We're badly outnumbered, and, unfortunate as it is to say, the French army is better equipped and trained for battle than us," Yassine stated.

"They've familiarized themselves with the landscape." said Sofiane.

"And they've had plenty of time to do so…well over a century," Karim replied.

They'd been driving at a modest speed in passing by farms, open fields of cattle grazing on vegetation, villages here and there, and, as Sofiane noted, "we're south of Tizi Ouzou." Amidst the Djurdjura mountain range, Sofiane appeared to be a bit nervous, looking at his rearview mirror, to his left and right, as well as over his shoulder.

"Is everything all right?" Djamila asked him.

"Look behind you. Do you see any cars nearby?"

Within a matter of seconds, she replied, "No."

Sofiane seemed to find what he was looking for at the base of a rugged mountain topped with snow at its peak, recklessly swerving off the highway and onto the rocky terrain. There were no vehicles, wildlife, people nor village in sight. No one else in the car said a word, allowing him to be in control. Several minutes had elapsed when Sofiane parked the car under an Atlas cedar tree, to which he also remarked, "there's a creek up ahead."

Out of the car, the four trekked on foot–not a trace of any footmarks nor even a footpath ahead in moving along the lush surroundings–until arriving at a cave. Its height was perhaps no more than fifteen feet. Sofiane reached for the flashlight tucked in his back pocket to light the way inside the cave, in lacking the supplies needed to assemble a makeshift torch. In addition, he handed Djamila his lighter. The four entered the dingy cave. For the time being, both the flashlight and the lighter were insufficient in what was still a rather dark cave, but the problem would be soon corrected. They came upon a large brown tarp on the floor, evident that contents were hidden underneath it.

On both sides of the cave rested two candle lanterns on the ground. Djamila lit the lanterns, providing the needed visibility. Sofiane looked around. "The guards are nowhere around," he said, almost to himself. He then removed the tarp, revealing a makeshift arms depot. Mortars, .50 caliber machine guns, hand grenades, ammunition; the weaponry was diverse. "*C'est incroyable*," Karim said, in effect to himself, having seen nothing like it, save for images shown in a film.

Yet, the quantity of arms on hand looked to be inadequate. *There must be more hidden arms depots*, Karim wondered, getting his hands on an assault rifle–the very first rifle he had ever clutched in his hands–placing it in an aiming position.

"Well, clearly the French haven't discovered this place," Sofiane said.

Karim carefully set the weapon down, right where he had picked up from, and moved over to Sofiane.

"These weapons were transported by sea via a Bulgarian ship, and landed off the coast of Morocco. We managed to successfully smuggle the arms across the border," Sofiane acknowledged.

"You went to great lengths to be able to hide these here, but *this is it*? I mean, surely more weapons were brought onto the ship?" Karim inquired.

"There were more weapons, without a doubt, but they've already been delivered into the hands of the ALN."

Sofiane handed the flashlight to Yassine and then pulled Karim to the side to give him a brief gunhandling tutorial; first with a revolver, and then a pistol.

Some shuffling noise emanated from outside, enough to alarm Sofiane. "Yassine, Djamila, go outside. See what all that noise is about," he said to them. As a protective measure, Yassine took hold of an assault rifle and trod gently, in case any intruders were lurking. Once outside, both scanned the immediate area, specifically on the lookout for the Commandos de Chasse, the French army's "Hunting Commandos," out to track down Algerian rebels, or any Algerian deemed to be suspicious. What was thought at first to likely be some shuffling noise from an animal, their efforts yielded two men approaching. It turned out both men were villagers, hired to guard the weaponry. They entered the cave, and went straight to Sofiane. "Please forgive us. We left to go eat," one of the men said.

"Make sure you stay put here until the soldiers arrive this evening to pick up the weapons," Sofiane replied.

"Understood. We'll be right here."

Sofiane turned to Karim. "You see, the smugglers were adamant about hiding the weapons in the mountains. When I became aware of this, it occurred to me that perhaps they were speaking from experience in handling the transport of arms in and around the Atlas Mountains, on the Moroccan side. The problem is though, this is not Morocco, of course."

"A wise choice to select this place for hiding, in my view."

"Listen, I don't want to spend any more time here. Let's get going," Sofiane said, then adding, "But I had to show you this place for yourself."

"And I'm glad I came to see this," Karim replied.

"Because eventually, you'll be called upon to transport weapons for armed combat."

One more stop remained, to a remote village some eighty kilometers to the southeast, in the direction of Bordj Bou

Arreridj. During the drive, Karim learned that Yassine was in fact the FLN's "Minister of Information," overseeing matters relating to the press, media, and public relations. Between the four of them, they shared snacks–walnuts, dates, apricots–inside the car. The drive led uphill and then a turn to a dirt road, passing by a plethora of citrus trees. The Mercedes pulled up to a small, brick farmhouse that really resembled more of a shack. About a half a dozen chickens were roaming around the front yard, which, like the road leading to it, was a dirt yard.

After parking the car, they made their way to the entrance. Approaching the door, Sofiane held his hand out, motioning to Djamila and Yassine to wait. "Hang out here. I'm just going to quickly show Karim the inside," he said.

Entering the house, it comprised of a kitchen without a dining table, a tiled living room area marred by stains and just filth in general, a sofa, a mini-drawer chest, a nightstand, a bookshelf, and lastly, half a bathroom–*sans une douche*. The windows from the inside completely concealed with curtains. Overall, Karim was rather impressed, compared to the apartment he resided in.

"Use this place as a hideout, a temporary place to stay, when conducting assignments," Sofiane said.

"I can consider it my home away from home," Karim responded.

"I'll be heading to China and the Soviet Union soon, so you'll be taking on greater responsibilities."

"That's what I'm here for."

Karim moved to a jar full of green olives on the kitchen counter. He popped the lid open and, once noticing that Sofiane wasn't looking in the same direction, fingered a good five olives out of the jar, and popping the olives, one by one, into his mouth. After the third, Sofiane took sight of it.

"Sorry, I couldn't say no," Karim said.

"Don't bother apologizing. Help yourself." Sofiane waited for Karim to finish. "I have trust in you, so here, take this: the key to the house," he said, handing it to Karim. The key was tucked inside Karim's front pocket, and Sofiane continued, "For now, let's make our meeting spot the tailor shop in Algiers. We can also exchange correspondence between the two of us through Amandine. Do stop by there daily. My wish is to see you complete some assignments first, before taking you to the clandestine FLN office in town."

"Understood. A practical, suitable way of conducting business."

"We try to avoid communicating via telephone, and the reason is obvious. But a telephone is available at the tailor shop when necessary."

Karim then took a peek out the front door to see Djamila and Yassine feeding the chickens pieces of bread, from the loaf of bread inside the car.

"Let's go to the back," Sofiane said, Karim following suit.

The back yard more or less resembled the front, apart from a few noticeable items: Numerous wooden crates, some broken, piled on top of one another, adjacent to a makeshift beige canvas awning. Underneath the awning, Karim came upon a vehicle: a white Volkswagen Beetle. At first sight, the exterior looked sharp; no signs of any damage or the like. He knew right away the car was for him, apparent as Sofiane drove a vehicle of his own. "Not the greatest, but it'll do the job," Sofiane mentioned.

"Wow, impressive! I'd be fortunate enough to even rent a car, much less own one," Karim remarked.

"You'll need the car to transport arms to different locations, among other duties. Or use it also for another purpose as you wish."

"Great, but I'll need to find a place to keep the car parked."

"Find a convenient and safe place. One that is not too far from home. Or, if it is rather far away, catch a trolley bus that will take you close to it."

Karim peered through the car windows, examining the interior. He spotted a newspaper in the backseat and a partially unfolded road map in the passenger's seat, an item that would come much in handy in accessing the highways throughout the country. Otherwise, the car was clean on the inside.

"With all the cross-country drives and back, wear and tear has taken somewhat of a toll. But the car is fine," Sofiane said.

"Nothing to complain about as far as I'm concerned. I am grateful for this."

Sofiane placed the car key square into his palm. "Oh, more will come, so long as you're committed to our cause. *L'algérie aux algériens.*"

Sound asleep in the mid-morning hour, Karim, who opted to spend the night prior at the farmhouse, was suddenly awakened by a commotion outside in the front, possibly a trespasser. He leaped off the sofa and immediately headed to the kitchen counter, scrambling through one of the drawers to retrieve a revolver. His first suspicion was that the trespasser was a French commando. If it was, he stood no chance by wielding a revolver compared to a soldier carrying an assault rifle, but nevertheless Karim reacted on impulse. Being as cautious as possible, Karim slid the kitchen window curtain ever so slightly, and his eyes spotted a lone man, though not sporting a military uniform of any kind whatsoever. His fear now assuaged to a moderate degree, he opened the front door and brought the revolver to an aiming position.

"Who are you?" he asked the man, bearded, dark-skinned, wearing a white burnous. Could this man be a *caid*? A tax collector, out to demand monies owed on the property?

"I'm so sorry. I don't want any trouble. I come in peace. But I am starving, and out looking for food. Have you anything I can eat?" the stranger replied.

The response pacified Karim, who withdrew the gun from the aiming position. "Just wait there. Don't move," he said. He went back inside the house, to the kitchen once more and grabbed a tall, slender jar of olives–different from the one he had been eating from–as well as a loaf of *kesra*, and brought it to the man. "Here."

"Many thanks." The man wasted no time in sinking his teeth into the bread.

"I don't know which way you came from, but are you not aware that there are fig and almond trees up the road over there?" Karim questioned. "They may not leave you with a full stomach, but at least it's something."

"Sir, I haven't the means to be picking fruits and nuts off tree branches. I'm fortunate I even have the ability to move about on foot."

"You've got some food now, now please leave!" Karim said, eager to move on. The man was on his merry way, back to wherever he'd come from.

February 21. After a sort of trial-and-error experiment, Karim settled with leaving the Volkswagen parked on Rue Levacher, at least for the time being. A small side street, away from any major boulevard, that was within walking distance from home. Other than a shop situated at the corner, adjacent to Rue Saint Augustin, it was a residential street, one that Karim felt safe in leaving the car.

A mild, yet mostly sunny day, he was on his way to Les Tailleurs Du Monde once more, the same place where Karim had first met Sofiane. Upon entering the tailor shop, he waited patiently as a client was picking up a pair of slacks. Karim sought to speak to Amandine Lévy, the Jewish woman who owned the shop. She stood behind the front counter, tending to the customer, and within minutes, it was Karim's turn to be helped.

"*Bonjour*, Madame Lévy. Remember me?" he asked.

"Why yes! It's Karim, isn't it?" Amandine replied.

"That's right. I'd like to speak to you in a private setting, if you don't mind?"

She wavered for a moment, buying herself some time to think about it. "Well, my office is in the back. We can go talk there. Let me get one of my employees to tend to the front counter. Hold on a minute." Amandine headed towards the rear of the shop and returned shortly, accompanied by a male employee who then idled by the counter.

"Follow me," she said to Karim.

Making their way to the rear, they passed by clothing racks to their left and right, holding men's suits, blazers, slacks and Islamic attire. Two wooden tables were littered with yarn, threads, needles, scissors, patches, epaulets and more. An employee was laboring behind a desk with a sewing machine; the clacking sound of the machine persisted as fabric was being stitched with a needle and thread. Les

Tailleurs Du Monde was a popular tailor shop where a fair amount of affluent clientele patronized it for their clothing alteration needs and was undoubtedly the busiest tailor shop in town. Amandine, surely in her late forties, give or take, was wearing a lavender dress, secured by a cord-like belt. A bit chubby in weight, her glistening jet black hair was tied into a bun. Of the many pieces of jewelry she wore on her wrists, fingers, ears and neck, the one that perhaps stood out above all was the gold Star of David necklace.

Leading Karim to the office, Amandine told him to wait again. Nothing lavish nor upscale about the office nor its contents; a steel metal tanker desk that showed its age and chairs that one would find in a school classroom. Amandine returned with two ornate cups filled with coffee, saucers underneath them.

"Care for some Turkish coffee?" she asked.

"Sure, of course," Karim replied, gladly accepting it.

Amandine took a seat on a swivel chair beside the desk, followed by a sip of the coffee. "Did Sofiane send you here?"

"Yes. He's the boss."

"Him and I go back several years. So what brings you back?"

Karim leaned back in the wooden chair. "I have a favor to ask you—one that will likely catch you by surprise. As I'm sure you know, Sofiane and I are part of the nationalist movement. No need to even mention the acronym. And, we need a place to store arms and other weaponry, and this is where we come to you for. We'd like to hide the arms here, at your place of business, provided you have the appropriate space to do so. Would you help us?"

"Oh my. No kidding, you were serious that this would catch me off guard," she replied, taken aback, and then placed the cup on the desk. "I'll need to take time to think about this."

"No rush," Karim replied, smooth.

"If you don't mind me asking, and please don't take this the wrong way, why don't you store the weapons at either his place, or your place? Just curious."

"Well, I live in the Casbah…–"

"Oh, that makes perfect sense," Amandine responded, cutting him off.

A shake of Karim's head, he then said, "I remember the Rue de Thèbes bombing as if it happened yesterday."

Her reaction mirrored his. "How can one forget that?"

"It's simply an inconvenient place, the Casbah, and unfeasible for us. The ascending and descending the stairs, the military checkpoints, it's susceptible to *ratonnades* and so on. Hence, we need to store the weapons in a place that is least likely to draw any sort of suspicion."

Amandine reached for the cup of coffee again, taking in a mouthful of the still-frothy drink. "I do have a brother who owns a textile factory just outside Tizi Ouzou. I think that would be a more ideal place to hide arms from the authorities, and I think he may accommodate you. Even more so by me convincing him."

Karim contemplated. "That's a possibility, and I'll relay that to Sofiane. But we're in need of a storage place here in Algiers. Whatever help you can provide will serve us greatly."

Amandine rose from her seat, and moved to the door, ensuring it was completely closed, but stopped short of locking it. She then reached for the wand tilt to shut the window's horizontal blinds for added privacy. Karim sensed that she was about to reveal some pleasing news to him. "Well, you may very well be in luck. I see what you,

26

Sofiane and the FLN are fighting for. And what I do have is storage space here, in the shop. Just out this door, to the left, a number of large, stuffed-to-the-brim cardboard boxes are concealing the storage space. It's secured with a padlock so that no employees can gain access inside, only me," she said.

"Wonderful!" Karim replied, appreciative. "That's just what we need. But I take it this is not the right time for me to take a look at it?"

"Oh no! I can only show it to you when my employees are not around. This will have to be done during off-business hours."

"Fair enough then. Would this evening do?"

"Sure, I can stay here later."

Karim's eyes focused in on her gold necklace, and, in a change of subject, he asked, "by the way, that Star of David necklace of yours, have you ever been chastised or experienced any hostility for wearing it?"

"Believe it or not, no. I haven't experienced any discrimination, any anti-Semitism due to my identity in Algeria."

"Good. May it continue to remain that way."

"My family and I left Paris in May of '40. Right at the opportune time, you can say. Call it foresight, if you will. We settled in Algeria and have been here ever since. But, as I'm sure you know, Jews have been in Algeria well before any of these European settlers ever set foot here."

Karim nodded his head. "Indeed. The roots run deep here. As for the settlers and their descendants, being entrenched in this land for as long as they have has shown no wholesale relinquishing of their control. *That* is evident. Sad as it is to say, I do see more turmoil, violence, and political instability on the horizon."

"Unfortunately."

"At any rate, you're a hard-working woman who does much service to this community and, moreover, a model citizen of Algeria."

"I'm pleased to hear that from such a young man as yourself."

"See you tonight."

Several hours had passed. Dusk settled in, and Karim arrived a bit earlier than expected on Rue Rovigo, despite the rush hour traffic. He sought to waste no time in heading to the tailor shop, fully aware that the business day had already ended and Amandine was giving up her personal free time in doing a favor for him. A throng hobnobbed in front of a nearby bar, likely awaiting entry to partake in an *apéritif*. Sure enough, Amandine was waiting in front of the entrance to the tailor shop.

"Bless you for waiting for me," Karim said to her.

"Just as I promised," she replied. "Come with me." Amandine led him inside and then past the counter, towards the other end of the establishment. Along the way, Karim sidestepped scattered remnants of cut up cloth, yarn, threads and the like that lay on the floor, the messy result from the labor of a long day's work. Amandine, used to such a sight on a daily basis, just walked over the scraps as if she or another employee would tend to it at a later time.

"So, what should I be expecting?" she asked.

"Handguns, assault rifles, grenades and the like," Karim replied. "The quantity of course depends on the storage size."

"As you say, young man. It's all foreign to me as far as I'm concerned."

Walking past a few clothing racks on both sides, Amandine led him to a mountain of cardboard boxes, piled one on top of another. Karim guessed that each one was approximately two feet in height, as well as length and width, and sensed that behind the boxes was the storage space that was concealed. To his left was what appeared to be a supply room.

"The storage space is behind these boxes," Amandine said. "Now comes the hard part–moving all of these boxes out of the way, because they are heavy, and I *do* mean *heavy*."

Karim placed both of his hands on one of the boxes above to get a better feel for its weight. "No kidding, it is," he muttered to himself.

"I'd personally give you a hand myself, but being a woman, my physical strength here is lacking," Amandine added.

"No worries, I'm more than able to handle this," he replied. "It just may take a while."

"Take your time."

Straight to the task at hand, Karim began toppling each box above, one by one, pausing for a break here and there, though barely breaking a sweat. He guessed that the contents inside the boxes were a combination of clothing, tools and equipment, perhaps abandoned or unwanted sewing machines and the like. For being the lean teenager that he was, Karim found the work to be quite laborious to say the least. In the meantime, Amandine had excused herself, periodically returning to check on the status. Karim carried on, until arriving at the last box remaining that rested on the floor. He waited until she returned once more.

"Well done," Amandine said. "Let's get this door unlocked." She moved to the door, a set of keys in one hand and a flashlight in the other, and unlocked the padlock, swinging the door wide open. She then handed the flashlight to Karim, who entered inside. The storage space was stuffy, to the point where Karim took a couple of steps back. Pointing the flashlight all around, he inspected the space to get an idea of its size, which, he felt, more resembled that of a large closet. There were no material objects–just empty space all throughout. Karim stepped out and Amandine turned to him.

"What do you think?" she asked.

"It's sufficient," Karim replied. "I'm satisfied with it."

"When do you plan on transporting the arms here?"

"At this point, I really don't know. It's not my decision, and we have to work out the logistics of it. But rest assured, I will let you know once I find out. You may even find out from Sofiane before me."

"Well, I'm always here."

"*Merci*, Madame Lévy. Should there be anything you need, I'll be there for you."

Rue Michelet and Rue d'Isly were both vibrant streets, full of life. The early settlers elegantly designed and fashioned the streets in the Haussmann-style of architecture. Beyond the high-end shops, one would find students at the many cafés, often arriving right after school for a beverage, seated outside on the sidewalk, often smoking a cigarette and chatting with classmates under the Mediterranean sun. On the one hand, it bemused Karim, in the manner in which Europeans flocked here and established themselves, in essence mimicking the lifestyle they had back in Europe, by silently proclaiming *this is our Cannes or Nice in north Africa*.

Karim made a stop at La Grande Poste d'Alger, the city's main post office, to purchase a money order, as well as several stamps, tucked into a glassine envelope. He then was on his way to the coastal suburb of Aïn Taya to deliver payment to an Algerian man who provided translation services; a man who also had contacts with the United Nations. He drove through the hustle and bustle that was Rue Michelet and continued on. Approaching Aïn Taya–Karim had to have been no more than five kilometers away–there appeared to be a roadblock of some sort in the distance. Drawing closer, it looked to be more of a checkpoint. Karim slowed down–it was too late to turn around and head back the way he came from as it would prompt suspicion.

When Karim came to a stop, three men were to his left–two police officers and the other, a soldier. "Where are you headed to?" one of the police officers inquired, a somewhat stocky figure, clean-shaven.

"Aïn Taya," Karim replied.

The officer shifted his eyes to the passenger's side of the vehicle. "Is this car yours?"

The soldier–a tall, blond figure with the stereotypical military haircut–carried an assault rifle that was secured by a sling that strapped over his shoulder. He now moved to the back seat window, peering through it, eliciting a split-second look over the shoulder by Karim, before responding, "Yes. This car was given to me. What is this checkpoint all about?"

"Public safety. May I see your driver's license?" the officer requested. Meanwhile, the other police officer just idled by and watched.

"I don't have one."

"So you're driving unlicensed...your age?"

"Seventeen."

It seemed as though the officer had encountered this

scenario many times before, and was unmoved in his demeanor. "Let me see the vehicle registration."

Karim opened the glove compartment. In searching through the contents, there in fact wasn't much: a screwdriver, a plier, and a few documents, but none of them were the vehicle's registration. "I don't see it. It's not here."

The officer let out a sigh. "*Descendez.*"

Karim muttered profanity to himself.

"*Descendez de la voiture tout de suite*," the officer repeated. *Get out of the car right now.*

Karim did so, and likewise, put his hands behind his back when ordered to, followed by being handcuffed. The soldier entered the car, searching both the front and backseat. He exited within moments with a newspaper in hand, showing it to the police officer. The officer reached for it with both hands, giving it a glance. "Ah, *El Moudjahid*. Reading material for scum like yourself!" he said to Karim.

Insulted, the remark agitated Karim, all the while being in a helpless position. As such, he did and said nothing, standing still under the sun.

The police officer then ordered the soldier to check the trunk. He popped it open, searching its contents. The soldier soon uncovered some items in the trunk. "Look at this," he said to the officer, showing him an assemblage of wires, cables, a roll of duct tape, as well as a timer. "They were underneath the trunk board." He then turned to Karim. "Are these materials for a bomb?"

"I don't know anything about that, sir." Karim's response was apparently unconvincing to the two men. He then added, "I'm telling you the truth. I've never even lifted the trunk board before."

The explanation was futile; in vain. The two men just weren't buying it. His wrists bound by handcuffs, Karim was now led to the back seat of a police vehicle, soon on his way to the police station.

The *commissariat de police*, police station, was located on 14 Boulevard Baudin, on a street known for being the home to financial institutions. Karim vowed he would admit nothing, flat out deny to the authorities any involvement in the FLN if interrogated about it. He knew the consequences would be severe if he were to make an admission, and knew it was best to say nothing. Upon entry into the police station, Karim was taken into a small, chilly room, without doubt an interrogation room, and the same police officer was accompanied by a pudgy man, sporting a dress shirt, suit, slacks, tie and a pencil mustache, surely an investigator. Once the officer departed, the investigator took the lead. He tossed the manila file folder he was holding onto the steel table. Making himself comfy in his seat, the man examined the first page, getting right down to the matter at hand.

"Driving unlicensed, *hein?*" the man commented.

"I took a risk. A reckless decision on my part," Karim answered.

"And no car registration papers?"

"I don't have an explanation for it, sir. The car was given to me, as a gift. I did not steal it."

"By whom?"

"A businessman." *A lie.* "Out in the *bled*. Someone who sympathized with me, being disadvantaged."

"So you're seventeen?"

"Yes."

"What do you know of bombmaking?"

"Nothing, actually."

"*Bicot*, how are you going to get me to believe that you had bomb paraphernalia in the trunk of your car and you knew nothing about it?"

"As I told the police officer, I had never even lifted the trunk board before. I've only driven the car just a few times, in fact."

"Are you a part of, or involved in, any revolutionary, insurgent, separatist groups or activities?"

"*Non, pas du tout.* I'm just a student."

"Not even the FLN?"

"No. I'm aware of what they stand for, but to answer your question, I'm not affiliated with them." *Another lie.*

The investigator rose from his chair. "Well, my work here is done." He then looked at Karim straight in the face. "You'll be escorted to your next destination."

Karim sought an explanation. "Which is?"

"Barberousse Prison."

A sick, nauseating feeling crept in the pit of Karim's stomach, to the point where he nearly vomited. He'd heard stories of FLN militants and operatives being incarcerated at the Barberousse Prison. But more than mere imprisonment, stories also of inmates being guillotined. But could one suffer such a fate for driving unlicensed? Or driving a "stolen vehicle," if that's how the authorities construed it? Surely *not*, Karim told himself. Or, what about involvement in "terrorist activities" by the discovery of "bomb paraphernalia," as the investigator described it? Now *that* seemed more likely. Yet, perhaps Karim was overreacting emotionally.

The police car entered the prison through the tall, palatial-like gate of double steel doors. Exiting the vehicle,

Karim was led through the courtyard, where the guillotine was in plain sight. The gut-wrenching feeling only amplified the moment he laid his eyes on the guillotine. Karim was then taken to an upstairs cell, accessible via a spiral staircase, by two prison guards.

Confined within such a small space, four walls surrounding him, a mattress on the floor and a pillow were the only tangible items inside. A firm pull of the locked door from the inside was futile. As the late night passed, and into the early morning hour, Karim couldn't sleep, a first for him. But, the bright news for him, so he told himself, was reminding himself of being informed that his prison stay would only last for one day. But even he had no idea what would transpire until then.

At nine o'clock in the morning, the sound of a key being inserted into the keyhole of the door awakened Karim immediately, causing him to rise up from lying on the mattress. Indeed, it was the same prison guard who led him into the cell–tall, pale-skinned, medium build in weight, black hair not much visible due to sporting a brown *kepi* that matched his uniform color–accompanied by another guard. Hunger and thirst kicked in for Karim, having not eaten nor drank anything in close to 24 hours. In fact, he hadn't even been offered any food nor drink since entering the prison's premises. When Karim made a kind request to the officers for food and drink, he was met with a cold, curt response of "This is not the time for that."

The prison guard turned to the other to consult with him. Speaking just above a whisper, he uttered, "So, what do you say? La *gégène*?" *Gégène*, the French military slang word for electroshock torture.

"He's just a kid," the second guard, a much younger counterpart, responded. "Save that for the adult men."

The first guard turned away, and dipped his head. He had to think about it, contemplating his decision. "Yeah, we do typically save the *gégène* for adult men. Let's opt for the next plan."

Both guards took hold of Karim, handcuffed him and led him out the steel door, down the hallway and into another room. From the moment Karim's eyes made contact with the water trough, he knew exactly what the guards had in store for him. The younger guard dragged a sturdy wooden bench, one end adjoining the trough, in order to elevate Karim and thus make it easier to plunge his head into the trough. The trough had to be at least five feet wide and three feet in length, pretty much filled to the brim with water that Karim imagined had to have been ice cold. Moreover, the water was somewhat soiled; discolored. Surely not clean water in any way, Karim said to himself.

As the older guard gripped the back of Karim's shirt and the other reaching for his feet, Karim resisted, but to no avail. He was thrown to the floor, endured a couple of kicks to the abdomen, as well as a blow to the face with a baton. Karim was defenseless, as his hands remained behind his back, bound by handcuffs. This time, Karim succumbed, and the guards lifted him off the floor and set him on the bench, knees resting on the bench, positioning him to where Karim's head was above the trough. The older guard put both his hands on the back of Karim's neck. "*Sale raton!*" he said to Karim's ear, a derogatory racial slur, before dunking Karim's head into the frigid water in the trough. With all his might, Karim attempted to lift his head but was unable to, as the strength of the guard's hands pressing against the back of his neck was too much to overcome.

Some sixty seconds passed, perhaps more, and the guard pulled Karim's head up and out of the water. Karim barely let out a gasp, releasing a couple of coughs, before his head was plunged into the water once more. This time though, water entered his mouth and trickled its way inside his body. His head still submerged underwater, this second plunge seemed longer than the first, and Karim wondered if he might lose his life due to a lack of oxygen. To his relief, the guard pulled his head up and out of the water once more, yet immediately threw him to the floor. Desperate for breath, repeatedly gasping and coughing, Karim hardly had time to recover. Both guards grabbed him firmly, lifted him off the ground, and led him out of the room, on the way out of the prison. If Karim uttered any words at them, it would only result in further physical abuse, he thought. After a police officer opened the gate's double steel doors, the same two prison guards uncuffed Karim's hands, releasing him, though it did not come without him enduring more kicks and blows with a baton, causing him to fall to the ground.

"Beat it, *sale raton!*" the older guard exclaimed. "We don't want to see your face ever again–either here or elsewhere!"

Thankfully, home was just a short walk away from the prison. As distraught as Karim felt, all he desired at that moment was to go home and to clear his mind, to the best of his ability, but above all, to seek that place of sanctuary (behind closed doors), a repose from the outside world. He was hell-bent on getting revenge; on "evening the score" in some fashion, but what? And how?

The routine passage through the labyrinth streets of the Casbah followed. Iznik tiles on some of the walls, intricately designed with floral patterns in turquoise as well as other colors, a remnant of the Ottoman Turkish conquest many centuries earlier. Children playing soccer on the pavement, kicking the ball back and forth to one another. On occasion, Karim would join in, providing some amusement to the kids in being the 'big brother' on the block. However, he was not in the mood at the time, and just walked by.

Karim arrived at the front door of his apartment, on Rue N'Fissa. From the moment he set foot inside, Karim sensed the tranquility. No one appeared to be home–not his siblings, nor mother. On the kitchen table was a plate of fried eggplant slices, next to a homemade jar of *harissa*. Karim reached for a slice, a bit on the cold side, but went ahead and added a dollop of *harissa* and ate it anyway. In no time, he finished the rest.

At the other end of the table, he laid his eyes upon a piece of mail–an envelope. Reaching for it, he saw that it was addressed to him. Yet, no return address was listed. Who could the sender be? Sofiane? Impossible, as Karim never revealed his address to him. The *lycée's* principal? Perhaps a desperate plea for Karim to reconsider and resume his studies to complete graduation? That was more likely. Karim could think of no one else. The envelope bore an Algérois postmark, though that didn't yield any further clues. He slid his finger through the envelope's flap, breaking the seal, and eagerly took hold of the contents inside–a letter, one on beige stationery paper. The letter was typed, and without a letterhead, but lowering his eyes revealed that it was written by Professor Didier.

March 1

Dear Karim,

This is Professor Didier. I hope you've been doing well the past two months. Your presence has been greatly missed in class. That being said, this is not the purpose of my letter to you. I'm writing to you because a dear friend of mine will soon be getting married to a young, beautiful Algerian woman, and I've been given permission to extend an invitation to you as I spoke very highly of you to Marco and Meryem. The wedding will take place on Saturday, April 29, out in the Mitidja. Among those who will be in attendance are businessmen, union leaders, city officials, and so forth. In short, this is a golden opportunity for you to possibly meet someone who may be beneficial to you and your cause. At any rate, the event would present an ideal occasion for us to reconnect, and my sincere hope is that you will view this in the same manner and attend the wedding. If interested, please let me know and I can send you further details, including the exact location of the venue. Stay safe and out of trouble, and as a friendly reminder: You can always send me correspondence to the school and be assured that I will read it.

Cordially,

Professor Didier Cachot

Karim handwrote a letter in Arabic and dropped it off at the tailor shop, intended for Sofiane. He described the details of the torture he endured, and vowed a "revenge" attack of some sort. In addition, Karim demanded that Sofiane bring "a bomb–one that will detonate without difficulty" while requesting that they meet a few days later, but this time at a different location: Avenue du 8 Novembre.

March 7. Karim was set to meet up with Sofiane, in what

had been weeks since the last time they'd seen each other. He thought about the letter Professor Didier had written to him. As much as Karim wanted nothing to do with Europeans, still angry and vindictive over undergoing torture at the prison, he was still too close to Professor Didier, a confidant to him, to simply write off the invitation and, in effect, give a "no" response. The good thing was that the wedding was not scheduled until the final week of April, so it gave Karim plenty of time to contemplate his decision.

It was another beautiful day with clear skies; spring was just around the corner. Karim left home and was on his way, making the descent of the flight of stairs that was characteristic of the quarter he lived in. It became standard protocol by now for him and Sofiane to meet at various locations throughout the city, for their own best interest, and safety. The checkpoints within the Casbah instituted by the French military only reinforced their belief that it was unwise to meet there.

After stopping by the local Moorish café in the Lower Casbah for a cup of coffee, Karim reflected on the insulting remark the *flic* made about *El Moudjahid* newspaper while being handcuffed, and it suddenly dawned on him as to how he would seek to exact his revenge: an attack on *L'Écho d'Alger*, the city's right-wing, ultra-conservative newspaper, and the most influential newspaper of the European settlers. Tit-for-tat, as far as Karim was concerned. And so it came, the perfect timing for him to discuss with Sofiane and plot how to carry out the attack.

The agreed meeting point at Avenue du 8 Novembre was too close to the *lycée*, so Karim took an alternate route on foot to arrive at the destination to avoid being seen by any former classmates or school officials roaming within the vicinity of the school. Finding himself on this street that was the headquarters to several public and private entities, Karim had a short wait until Sofiane pulled up to the curb in his Mercedes. He got in the car, pleased to have a friend at his side to talk to. Djamila was sitting in the backseat.

"You took quite a beating, eh?" Sofiane asked him.

"Oh God, it was nerve-racking," Karim replied. "The water torture, but, you know, it could have been a lot worse. I somehow managed to avoid being electroshocked."

"You really dodged a bullet with that one. I mean that figuratively. But are you OK?"

"I'm fine, I suppose."

"Don't feel like you're the only one. As you know, I'm no stranger to being locked up in prison."

"And who knows what has happened to the car. It's safe to assume that the cops, the authorities, seized it and now claim it as their own property."

Sofiane turned the corner onto the next street and reached into his shirt pocket for a cigarette pack, still wrapped in cellophane. "Let them keep the fucking car."

Karim looked to his left to face him, bewildered by what he'd just heard. "What? How can you say something like that?"

"The vehicle isn't even mine to begin with. It belongs to the owner of the farmhouse, who has since been deceased. I put fraudulent license plates and hid the vehicle registration so that the *flics* couldn't trace the vehicle back to our hideout."

"Clever. But gee, I wish I'd known that while being interrogated by those damn *flics*. It would have saved me a lot of stress and anxiety."

"Some things are best kept secret."

"But still, I'm going to need a vehicle when doing missions out of town."

"It'll be in the works. Hopefully we can get you another one soon."

"So, what happened to the owner of the farmhouse? How did he die?" Karim inquired.

"A heart attack," Sofiane replied curtly. "And I knew the man personally, one whom I had a warm friendship with, so don't suspect that it was anything sinister."

Karim stuck his right arm out the passenger's window, the cool, crisp breeze blowing right by as they cruised along the seafront there on the Boulevard de la République. The Bay of Algiers was only a stone's throw away as the fish market, La Halle aux Poissons, lay at the quay. All the while, Djamila remained silent, respectfully allowing the two men to carry on in their conversation.

"I'm sorry you had to endure this, but answer me this: Are you upset now?" Sofiane asked Karim.

"I'm angry," Karim replied. "And I'm out for revenge."

"Good. And where do you plan on carrying out your revenge?"

"*L'Écho d'Alger.*"

"Excellent choice," Sofiane said, exhaling a puff of smoke. "And we have on hand something that will put that place in shambles–a bomb. All I have to do is activate the timer, which takes little effort."

"Wonderful. Are you comfortable in tinkering with a bomb?"

"Of course. Consider me experienced." Sofiane then added, "And Djamila will be accompanying you. You've got everything, Djamila?"

"Yes, I have the wig and the purse to hide the bomb in," Djamila replied. She was sporting a classy summer dress, typically worn by the chic French ladies in town, as well as sunglasses and a straw bonnet cap. The scarlet red lipstick was not characteristic of such worn by the average Muslim woman.

Sofiane turned onto Rue Arago and parked the car, discussing with them the plan of action to be taken. His intuition at work, he pulled out a piece of paper and an empty envelope from a leather padfolio, writing down a message intended for the newspaper's editor-in-chief in also revealing the man's name: Fabrice Buisson. It was apparent that Sofiane had a fair amount of knowledge of *L'Écho d'Alger*, including the names of at least one of its employees.

"Hand me the bomb," he then said to Djamila. She handed it to him with care. As Sofiane tinkered with setting the timer, Djamila and Karim idled inside. In due time, he stated, "ten minutes," in reference to the time remaining in which the bomb would detonate. Meanwhile, Djamila put and then adjusted the blonde wig on her head and took one last look into her handheld mirror, appraising her appearance. Sofiane handed the bomb back to her, along with the letter tucked inside the envelope, and she placed them inside her purse.

"You remember the protocol?" Sofiane asked her.

"Yes," Djamila replied.

His eyes narrowed in on the watch on his left wrist. At precisely ten minutes after one o'clock in the afternoon, he said, "Seven minutes. Go!"

Karim and Djamila darted out of the car and were on foot. Walking arm-in-arm like two lovers on this arcaded street, they passed a hotel and then turned the corner ahead, which led them to *L'Écho d'Alger*, located at 20 Rue de la Liberté. Upon entering the building, both headed straight to the receptionist's desk, occupied by a young, nerdy-looking man who appeared to be in awe of the beauty of Djamila, or rather, the façade of her disguised as a chic French woman.

"Good afternoon. I am here to drop off this letter to the editor-in-chief, Fabrice Buisson," Djamila said to him, handing the letter to him.

"Sure. I believe he is on lunch break. I can hold onto it until he returns."

"Can you please just drop it off at his desk? The letter is of an urgent matter."

"Yes, I can go ahead and drop it off inside his office upstairs. I'll be right back."

"I'll wait here until you're back," she said, lying to him.

As soon as the receptionist was out of sight, Karim moved to Djamila and spoke into her ear in a tone above a whisper, in Arabic, "Put the purse under the desk! *Yalla!*" Hurry!

Djamila bent her knees and placed the purse on the floor, then sliding the purse under the desk with her foot. They both turned around and, in a calm, cool manner, casually left the scene to avoid eliciting any suspicion from any employees in sight. Once back out on the street, they picked up the pace, essentially speed walking and, as soon as they turned the corner, back to Rue Arago, ran straight to the car where Sofiane remained. Both of them hopped inside the car. "Success!" Karim said.

"Don't say that yet! I want to see or hear the explosion!" Sofiane retorted. He immediately started the engine and hit the gas pedal. Approaching the intersection, he slowed down and then came to a full stop amidst crossing traffic, uttering profanity in being momentarily delayed. Yet, in next to no time, Sofiane recklessly swerved a left turn onto Rue de la Liberté.

"Pull over!" Djamila uttered.

Sofiane did so right away, and parked the car, though the engine was still running. All three of them turned their heads over their shoulders in anticipation of the explosion. No more than twenty seconds elapsed and they saw and heard the chaos that ensued as the bomb exploded, wreaking havoc on the building that housed the newspaper outlet. Pedestrians of all sorts took off in a frenzy, struck with fear, yet at the same time, avoiding personal harm or injury. Sofiane put the car's shift out of the parking gear, and drove off. Karim turned his head over his shoulder once more, and holding up his index finger, said, "Round one."

II

The destruction caused–a prominent media outlet reduced to shambles, would surely add only more fuel to the fire for the remaining pro-French Algeria press. Yet, Karim held his head up high. No remorse. Nevertheless, he had to skip town, at least for some time, and head far away from the environs. The fear of a *ratonnade*–a racial attack on one of Algerian or Arab descent–for him, or any young Algerian man who fit the profile of a troublemaker, was all too great, so he believed. With Sofiane at his side, a several-hour drive commenced from Algiers to the Aurès mountains in eastern Algeria.

Taking an alternate route, one that led them through the lush landscape of Greater Kabylia, Sofiane couldn't help but to share his thoughts on the attack. "That's the last of that right-wing rag," he said.

"But we shouldn't think that that will be the end of

hearing, and reading, more pro-colonialism propaganda," Karim replied.

"Right you are. There are other outlets of course. *L'Écho d'Alger* may have been the biggest mouthpiece, but rest assured others will step up and fill that void in reverberating their voice. I like to think of it as tit-for-tat. We lost our FLN publication in Algeria, basically through exile via threats and force, and now the pro-colonialists lost one of theirs, by our own hands, which we should take great delight in."

"Indeed. But I'd hate to learn, or even see with my own eyes, my mug featured in one of the other local papers. A manhunt for me." Karim shook his head at the thought of it.

"Don't think that. Don't even let that penetrate your mind. By escaping town for a few weeks, perhaps even a month at least–the more time passes, slowly but surely, such a manhunt will gradually diminish and fade away."

"Agreed. I need to avoid Algiers for a while."

The Aurès mountains were ahead of them. As Sofiane pointed out, the region was a haven for the FLN and the rugged terrain made that quite apparent to Karim. Sparse, minimal signs of life present, this land was suitable for the Imazighen, or Berbers, the indigenous people of North Africa, living there. It seemed like a world away from the hustle and bustle of Algiers, Karim thought. The nearest town was dozens of kilometers away–Khenchela. Being in the interior of the country, far away from the coast, the heat was not stifling that day, but bearable. Sofiane diverted off the main highway and later drove towards a rocky hill to which he drove around to the other side of it. He found what he was looking for and parked the car next to a small number of short shrubs before getting off.

Both men came to a makeshift camp that had been set up. Wooden tables and bench seats were arranged, connected in a line, and alongside five women were preparing meals in what was, for all intents and purposes, an outdoor kitchen. Moreover, a multitude of men in military uniforms were present, taking instruction and orders from one of their superiors. To Karim, this was without question the ALN, *Armée de Libération Nationale.*

A short, stocky man parted from the assemblage and approached Sofiane and Karim. The man had a pudgy face, at least a day's long stubble of a beard, sporting a pale turtle color of a uniform. He stopped within feet of both men and did the customary army salute, to which both men reciprocated. "Sofiane, you made it." He turned to Karim, "And who do we have here?"

"This is Karim," Sofiane replied.

The man extended his hand for a shake.

"The youngest and most dangerous of Algeria's revolutionaries, and a recent track record to prove it," Karim replied, confident, pompous, boastful, meeting his hand for the shake.

The remark elicited laughter from both Sofiane and the chubby man. "Don't be so cocky," Sofiane said.

"I don't mind. I like this young man already," the army man responded. "As for me, Colonel Lotfi Khedim, commander of Wilaya 1. Follow me."

Colonel Lotfi led the way, soon introducing Karim and Sofiane to the soldiers. The men sported army caps and were all, as far as one could see, in shape. As Karim quickly noted, the age range of the soldiers varied, from late teens or so to middle-aged men. But an intuitive feeling struck Karim that the men were out of sync. The commands given by the colonel were followed by missteps in motions and movements from the soldiers. Was there a lack of comprehension through a language barrier? Were the soldiers simply poorly educated in military training or tactics? Or a bit of both? Karim said nothing, for now at least, aware that it would be impolite to remark on such in front of the army. He observed the men for perhaps no more than fifteen minutes, and then moved to the cooking area.

The five female cooks, all Imazighen women of the Chaoui tribe, did not do much chatting with one another, Karim noticed. It was more of a strict focus on the job at hand, perhaps for fear of being scolded for socializing that might be deemed excessive. He was set to go against any unwritten rule of the kind and strike a conversation with at least one of the women. All wore traditional colorful tunics—from red, blue, yellow and more—as well as headpieces of jewelry. The aroma from the cooking inside the cauldron hinted of grains, accompanied by what looked to be offal, visible on the skewers cooked over an open fire.

Karim approached one of the women nearest to him. "A Berber specialty?"

The woman gave a sort of wry smile. "Not even on the best of days. We're always short on food supplies, and with all the men we have to feed, we have to make the meals stretch with the most economical of ingredients."

"Grains and legumes always seem to do the trick," he replied.

"Of course. We have cooked barley here, which will be topped with the chicken liver you see on the skewers, and garnished with sautéed almonds. A relatively simple meal, and not many ingredients needed to prepare it," the woman said, who gave her name as Lila.

"By the gracious, benevolent hands of God, you and

the other cooks have been able to get your hands on food supplies."

"Not long ago, three men in a camion brought us kilos of food supplies: sacks of grains, legumes, root vegetables, and tins of canned tuna and sardines."

"Surely that didn't last long."

"Nope."

"And in truth, who knows where those men got all those food supplies from? I have my doubts that the supplies originated from an Algerian farmer or producer."

"At the end of the day, does it even matter where it came from?"

"I suppose not."

"In times of war, the rules are tossed in the trash bin."

Sofiane approached Karim, who stepped away from Lila to chat in private. Looking towards the soldiers, Karim said to Sofiane, "I'm beginning to see why you chose me for this role."

"Why do you say that? Your education?" he replied.

"The soldiers just seem out of sync, which, to your point, is indicative of education, or lack thereof."

"I concur," Sofiane answered, "believe me, I've noticed. Here's the thing: much of these men have had very little, if any, schooling, much less formal instruction. They simply don't possess the intellect, shall I put it, of someone like you."

"Well that's reassuring."

"You are not needed in a military capacity, *that* is clear."

"Being from the city puts me at a huge advantage."

Within moments, Colonel Lotfi joined the two men.

"Have your hands full, Colonel?" Karim asked him.

"As always, vetting each man thoroughly. Not a fluid task as many of the men are illiterate," Lotfi replied.

"Yet obedient, wouldn't you say?" Sofiane chimed in.

"Agreed. That being said, I've instilled in them that the line has been drawn and there's zero tolerance for betrayal; any treasonous behavior. Better to detect any possible *harkis* right away."

"I fucking hate traitors."

"Yet, being disenfranchised and displaced, these men are more aligned with the love of *notre patrie*, our people and stand firmly with Algerian national identity. They're from rural areas and have a thorough knowledge of the mountainous terrain, which is a tremendous advantage to us."

"More recruits are on the way?" Sofiane asked him.

"I'll be meeting with dozens of them tomorrow."

The cooks announced the meal was ready to be served, with the colonel and soldiers queuing first, each helping themselves to a hearty portion. They then sat on the ground, bowl and spoon in hand. Sofiane and Karim followed suit. The soldiers gave a prayer prior to eating, ever so grateful for the meal, as did the others. Chatter continued, songs were sung, and the cooks were quick to clean up and pack equipment after the meal.

"It's time to leave from here. We don't want to be here any longer than we should," the colonel said.

The female cooks loaded the cookware and equipment into a military truck, as if a sense of urgency kicked in, it seemed. Karim offered to lend a hand.

"We need to cover up our tracks, in case the French army happens to search the area," Lila said to him.

Hearing this from one who wasn't a soldier nor in

military command, Karim inquired, "Have you heard any word of the French army heading in this direction?"

"I haven't, but we have to take extra precaution. We don't want to leave any trace of our presence here."

"Fair enough. Let's do our part."

The women, no doubt, had become accustomed to this, and it showed, carefully cleaning up the scene and leaving the surroundings as if no hint of activity was present. The ALN departed the scene, and Karim gave a verbal farewell, as well as waving goodbye for now. Colonel Lotfi shook his hand, certain he would see Karim again soon.

Karim moved towards the rear of the truck and Lila, before hopping onto the truck's bed, turned to him. "Best of luck to you in Algiers, Karim. Stay out of harm's way."

Karim spent the rest of the month out in the *bled*, the countryside, staying at the farmhouse. His assignments were rather minimal in nature during this time, mainly approaching locals to inquire of any interest on their part in wanting to join the ALN, or any skills or services that could be rendered to aid the cause, which was met with moderate success. At and around the property itself, Karim at times would climb fruit and nut trees and picked figs, almonds and more. Those he didn't eat right away, he stored for future use. He'd also feed the chickens that roamed in front of the house with the aid of local villagers, who taught Karim how to skin and butcher one as well. These were the rural survival skills that Karim would otherwise not acquaint himself with in the city, and he was grateful for all he'd learned.

When Karim returned home the first week of April, the letter from Professor Didier was on top of his bed, put there by his mother or one of his siblings as a reminder. The decision was made to accept the professor's invitation to the wedding, more due to feeling compelled not to let him down. *I'll be there. Please send me the address and details. See you soon*, Karim wrote on another piece of paper and then tucked into an envelope, to be dropped off at the post office.

The Generals' putsch in April had come to pass, resulting in failure, unsuccessful in the quest to oust Charles de Gaulle. The 1st Foreign Parachute Regiment seized Algiers, and, to no surprise, throngs of Europeans descended onto the streets, chanting "*Algérie française!*," distrustful of de Gaulle and his motives. For much this reason, Karim did exactly what Sofiane ordered him to do, which was to avoid the streets and stay at home, thus confining himself within the Casbah. Sofiane could not take the risk of potentially losing what became his closest associate; his 'partner in crime,' whether it be due to mob violence or even by arrest, and made the decision that was in the best interest. He stayed attuned to the events that transpired over several days by way of listening to a transistor radio. Just the very instance of Sofiane hearing that pro-French Muslims, or *Harkis*, were present amongst the flock of gatherers, made him cringe. In Sofiane's book, they were nothing more than traitors, a stain on Algerian pride, identity and nationality, and he believed that at some point—somehow, some way—the *Harkis* would be dealt with and face severe consequences for their treason.

On the part of the FLN, as far as they were concerned, the failed putsch only weakened the French position vis-à-vis Algerian self-determination, which they were confident would play right into their hands. As such, the FLN planned their strategies moving forward.

April 29. Not wanting to take another chance in driving a vehicle as an unlicensed driver and risk facing the consequences once more, Karim hired a chauffeur to drive him to the wedding venue with funds procured from Sofiane. And so it came, he was on his way to the wedding in the Mitidja–the vast plain located south of Algiers that stretched for dozens of kilometers. The chauffeur, a semi-retired man from El-Biar, drove with relative ease, and after a quick stop at a roadside farm stall to grab a bag of oranges, they arrived at a schoolhouse, where the wedding was located.

Getting out of the car, the heat was almost unbearable; rays of sunlight beaming down on Karim. An assemblage of guests were mingling with one another in front of the schoolhouse, a custard-colored building topped with a steeple, surely an elementary school for the children of this agrarian region. The area was also lined with rows and rows of wooden chairs for the guests. In the near distance, a number of parked cars that belonged to the guests and their chauffeurs. Karim wore the same exact outfit that was his school uniform–a stale navy blue blazer, white collared shirt and black slacks. He proceeded to the crowd, feeling a bit embarrassed that he arrived underdressed compared to the men he saw ahead of him, many of whom were sporting tuxedos. As for the female guests, they looked lovely in their white dresses.

It took some time, but Karim finally spotted Professor Didier walking out the door of the schoolhouse entrance, glass of champagne in hand, blending in with the horde of guests. Karim approached him, happy to see the man.

"So, did you invite me to talk me into returning to school again?" he asked, joking, a smile radiating across his face.

Didier laughed. "Of course not." He took a sip of champagne. "Though I wouldn't mind. So what's new? How's life been treating you?"

"Oh, it's been rough. The tricks of the trade. Learning new skills along the way. I've just got to stay out of trouble, you know."

"I hear of small groups of extremists popping up here and there, on the pro-colonialist side. For the safety of the general public, let's hope they don't spread like locusts. I don't say this to influence or even dissuade you from what you're doing, but just be careful out there."

"Noted," Karim replied, a nod of the head. "Well for now, ain't it grand to be out here, away from it all?"

"Admittedly, I need a break from the city life, and the Mitidja suits me perfectly."

The bride and the groom made their way through the crowd, striking up conversations with one guest after another. Eventually, they came to Karim and Didier, cordially introducing themselves, followed by the exchange of pleasantries. The bride, a tall, burly Genoese named Marco Tanzini, moved from Italy to Constantine years earlier to start his own dental practice. The groom, an olive-skinned, somewhat plump Oranese by the name of Meryem Boumendjel, had been gainfully employed as a *fatma*, or domestic servant.

"There's plenty of food available inside the schoolhouse. Help yourself," Didier advised Karim. He went right away, entering through the wide open double wooden doors, and was met with an exquisite offering of food, pleasing to the taste buds of both Europeans and North Africans alike: a leek and tomato quiche, a celery rémoulade, *méchoui*, and a pile of *feuilles de bricks* stuffed with ground chicken, others with eggs and tuna. To satisfy the sweet tooth, a tower of cream puffs known as *croquembouche*. Apart from the *croquembouche*, Karim helped himself to a hearty portion of each, a far cry from the meager diet he had been so accustomed to.

Leaving the scene, Karim returned to catch up with Didier to find that he was engaged in a lively discussion with an elderly couple. Didier was quick to introduce both of them, who were Spaniards, to Karim. "Here's someone I want you to meet–Sebastián Ruiz." Sebastián had sparse oily gray hairs atop an otherwise bald head. A stout figure, he sported a silver pair of slacks and suit over a white collared shirt. "And this is his wife, Claudia Ruiz," Didier added. She reached for a handshake from Karim. Her smile radiated upon meeting his eyes, and Karim sensed right away that she held a liking for him, which, unbeknownst to him or not, would work in his favor. A woman with jet black hair tied into a bun, in contrast to her white dress.

"I think the two of you may share something in common," Didier said, referring to Sebastián and Karim. "I'll leave both of you for now," he added, walking away.

"Didier has told me only little about you. What do you do?" Sebastián asked.

"Well, I'm rather ashamed to admit this to you, but I'm a high school dropout," Karim replied.

"Really? For what reason? Surely there must be good cause for doing so. Did you decide to pursue another endeavor?"

Karim looked around, realizing that he needed to speak in a low enough tone of voice for no one to over-hear. "I shouldn't be saying this, especially near a crowd surrounding us like this, but I'm a member of the FLN. Consider me an operative."

"A young man such as yourself? Impossible!" Sebastián uttered, a bit taken aback.

"*C'est la vérité*," Karim responded. *It's the truth.*

"Well, come to think of it, I shouldn't be surprised by it."

"Really? Why do you say that?"

Sebastián looked to his right and then looked over his left shoulder. He then motioned to Karim. "Let's move over to the lemon tree. We'll have a bit more privacy." They did so, right under the shade, now spared from the direct sunlight hitting them in the faces, and Sebastián continued, "The FLN needs all the help they can get. As I see it, they're badly outnumbered, and don't have enough equipment and wherewithal to successfully counter the French army."

"I'm realizing that more and more with each passing day. You seem to have at least a fair amount of awareness of the FLN and the current state of affairs. What else do you know?"

"Oh boy," Sebastián sighed. "I'll be glad to share it with you. I've had dealings with a few FLN operatives in the past. Given my profession as a lawyer, I've been approached in the past for my services in being able to represent them; to aid these men facing prosecution, imprisonment and so on. One of the men, Chérif Zerrouki, was a key figure in carrying out the All Saints' Day attack, back during the FLN's infancy. Any of this sound familiar to you?"

"Doesn't ring a bell to me," Karim replied.

"Surely not. You're still a kid. Think late '54, and '55, the early stages of the FLN. There's also been a little of, what I like to call 'underground' work I've been engaged in with the operatives. But I won't divulge into that here. Not to toot my own horn, but I'm a big-name lawyer in Algiers, and have connections with high-profile individuals in the city, and the whole of Algeria for that matter."

"Looks like I've come across the right man; a blessing that I've stumbled upon today. I have a request to make, Monsieur Ruiz: As I'm sure you may know, the FLN is seeking to expand its influence and effectiveness, and I'm confident that my superior would be delighted at the opportunity to discuss how you may be of assistance to him. Would you be willing to take the time to meet him?"

Sebastián wavered at first, only to later shrug his shoulders. "Sure, why not?"

"Wonderful!" Karim responded.

The two men were suddenly sidetracked by an announcement that the wedding ceremony was moments away from commencing. Once seated, the guests' attention shifted to the bride and groom. In due time, a minister stood before them. Following the recital of vows, the minister concluded by issuing the official proclamation of Marco and Meryem as husband and wife. The guests erupted in applause, with several waiting around to personally congratulate and speak to the newlyweds. Quite the festive scene no doubt, and as Karim was heading inside the schoolhouse, Sebastián approached him. "Before I leave, here's my business card. You'll find me at my office. Stop by, and let's talk. It was a pleasure to meet you," he said, handing the card to Karim.

"Likewise, Monsieur Ruiz. You'll be hearing from me and my associate soon."

Sebastián and Claudia left the scene. Karim wiped beads of sweat off his forehead and headed inside the schoolhouse for a glass of non-alcoholic apple cider, taking a sip while standing about a meter from the wicker cart carrying champagne bottles and other bottled beverages. A young, olive-skinned woman with long brunette hair caught his eye, to the point where his eyes were fixated on her. Shortly, Didier joined Karim and he could sense what Karim was focusing on. "Glad you came?" Didier asked him.

"Indeed I am," Karim replied. "You were right."

"About what?"

"Networking with others. Looks like I've found someone who will be to my favor."

"I knew it. You took my word for it, and it's working out for you. I'm heading back home."

"I'll get a ride with you. The chauffeur is long gone. Just give me five more minutes."

"I'll wait for you in my car." Didier moved closer to him and spoke in a low tone, near Karim's ear, "By the way, don't flirt with the French ladies. They're all taken." Didier grinned before walking away.

Sofiane was upbeat, eager at the prospect of meeting Monsieur Ruiz. He remained rather vague to Karim on what topics he wanted to discuss with the lawyer. In any case, it involved money. *That* Karim did know. The two left Square Nelson in the late morning hour by car, and ventured into Bab-el-Oued–the European stronghold; a middle-class neighborhood that was heavily Spanish. As such, to a great extent, Sofiane viewed it as entering "enemy territory." Of grave threat to both men, and to the Algerian independence movement for that matter, was the recent formation of the OAS, *Organisation Armée Secrète*–composed of fringe right-wing pro-colonialists who sought to preserve *Algérie Française* by any means necessary, which undeniably included violence. In essence, to prevent

Algerian independence. Their non-physical presence was made known through posters affixed to buildings and walls daubed in graffiti with various slogans and the like. Among them: "*OAS*," "*OAS VAINCRA*," "*OAS VEILLE*."

Sebastián's law office was located on Avenue des Consulats. A tramway ran along this street, hence Sofiane parked elsewhere. He and Karim soon arrived at the address and ascended the stairwell to the second floor. After hearing the knock on the door, the receptionist, a young, blonde French lady by the name of Mathilde Lavoie, opened it, welcoming them in. She led Karim and Sofiane from the main reception area and past the desk of the absent paralegal, and into Sebastián's office. Sebastián was quick to greet both men. The office–a comfy, cozy space that, in addition to the walls being adorned with plaques and framed images of Sebastián's educational and professional achievements, also featured framed photographs of various cities in Spain–Madrid, Barcelona and others. The window to the left was then closed by Sebastian. Sofiane and Karim took a seat on chairs in front of the executive desk, impressed by the office.

"Before we get started, I've got a bottle of anisette here and a carafe of homemade *sangría* that my wife brought this morning. What can I get both of you gentlemen?" Sebastián asked.

Karim turned to his left to look at Sofiane, deferring to him. *You answer this question for us.* Sofiane hesitated at first. "Well, we don't drink alcohol. Sorry, we have to respectfully decline. It's a religious thing to us."

"I figured you'd say that. But I had to ask anyway in not wanting to come across as being inconsiderate by not offering. So what brings you two here?"

"Well, perhaps we may have more than one request of

you, so it may be asking too much. But, to get straight to the point: As I'm sure you know, there are several thousands of Algerian workers in Paris. It has been our practice, the FLN's practice, of milking funds from the workers, which in turn has helped fund our operations. So what we desire is for an intermediary, a middleman, to move funds from Paris to Algiers, by a different means than the transporting of money into Switzerland via the Jeanson Network," Sofiane answered.

"Well, the Jeanson Network had a good run...who would've thought that it would suddenly crumble and completely fall apart?" Sebastián replied.

"Which is why we must find another means of getting ahold of the funds, one that will not cause the authorities or government to be suspicious. This is where we turn to you. Perhaps a close contact or colleague you know of in Paris who can assist us? We'd be ever grateful if you can help in any way."

Sebastián, sitting behind his desk, leaned back in his chair and clasped his hands on his lap, not saying a word, thinking of his next response.

"I'm cynical of de Gaulle," Sofiane added.

"As well you should be."

"I'm concerned that he's going to cave in to these right-wing fanatics, and the war will only be prolonged indefinitely...as if six-plus years hasn't been enough."

Sebastián remained silent for several seconds before uttering, "Let's see." He then rose from his leather executive chair and slowly moved to the window, as if buying himself time to brainstorm a list of names. The time that elapsed in silence indicated to Sofiane that he was about to receive a favorable response, he sensed. Sebastián turned away from looking out through the window, and said, "A former colleague of mine, an Algerian, is a lawyer at a respected law firm in Paris. The firm specializes in banking and finance, if I'm not mistaken. He's also well connected to the Paris Bar. His name is Sami Bekkouche. I can provide you his contact information."

"Excellent. This sounds very promising to me."

"He's transferred funds to my business' bank account before, so the question of me receiving funds here in Algiers won't be an issue."

"I'm pleased to hear that."

"I advise you not to telephone him, for obvious reasons. Better to either correspond with him via postal mail or to pay him a visit in Paris to arrange a meeting in private."

"Making a trip to Paris won't be an issue for me."

Karim, mum all this time, finally chimed in by adding another request. "Would you know anyone who can help with producing a phony driver's license? I was recently sent to prison and tortured due to driving unlicensed, something I didn't mention to you before."

"Karim, these people are ruthless in their treatment of prisoners, it's—"

"Oh, I experienced that firsthand," Karim replied, cutting him off.

"And believe me, you are not the only one. Far from it. Many ex-prisoners, Algerians of course, will relate by sharing similar accounts."

"It must be said, it turned out that I received a more lenient treatment because of my age."

"Well, you caught a break there. But nevertheless, for a great number of these colonialists in positions of power, a *raton* is a *raton*, regardless if it's a 90-year-old disabled man or a child. That's their viewpoint, sadly. I'm proud to say I don't share that sentiment. But, as someone of European descent, saying this to you is a way of shedding some light into the mindset of these '*ultras*,' as they're also called. Be thankful you didn't experience electroshock torture. You might not be around today had that been the case."

"I respect your stance on this, sir."

Sebastián took a gulp of his sangría. "Anyhow, back to the point," he said. He contemplated for a moment before continuing, "There's a good friend of mine, now retired, who was an ex-government employee of 30 years. During his career, he familiarized himself with creating fake identification documents, doing so in an underground capacity, even active in engaging in this activity during the Second World War. He's the right man to get the job done."

"And he's currently in Algeria?" Sofiane asked.

"Yes," Sebastián replied. He then turned to Karim. "Have you any photos on hand?"

Karim reached into his back pocket and pulled out a pair of passport-sized photos, placing them on the desk. "Until then, I can't be driving anywhere. Not even within the city, much less to the Mitidja, the mountains, or even across the country. I won't take that chance again."

Sebastián assured both men that he'd be working in their best interest, and, in turn, Sofiane and Karim graciously thanked Monsieur Ruiz, knowing they had a man whom they could rely on and trust.

May 10. Being aware of the OAS' existence and presence, Karim owed it to himself, and more importantly to the FLN, to delve further in extracting any information he could about the OAS from locals. Following the morning prayer at the Safir Mosque, Karim was on his way to the Marché de la Lyre to speak to a shopkeeper. En route, he strolled through the large arcades located on Rue de la Lyre, a street always bustling with Arab and Jewish merchants selling clothing, rugs, other housewares and more. Also, shoe shine boys eager to acquire clients and offer them a pristine shine despite the meager amount of payment received for services rendered.

Karim entered through the open doors of the market that was the Marché de la Lyre and straight to a stall that specialized in selling olives and jars of *harissa*, a place he started frequenting recently. The shopkeeper, Ahmed, a chubby man in his forties or fifties, with a shaved head and sporting a 5 o'clock shadow on his face, was born to an Algerian father and French mother. Ahmed had placed some jars on a shelf and then turned around to find Karim.

"Welcome back, Karim. You're now *un habitué* here," Ahmed said. A regular.

"You'll be seeing more of me in the future," Karim assured him.

"That's good news for me."

Karim reached into his left pants pocket and pulled out a 10-franc note, placing the bill on the glass counter. "Here. This is for your trouble."

Ahmed put his fingers on the note and slid it towards himself. "That is mighty generous of you, young man. But what for?"

Karim leaned on the glass counter. "So tell me, what do you know about the OAS?"

"I can't say I know a whole lot about them."

"Anything said from any of your customers? Any word from out on the streets?"

"Nothing, really," Ahmed said, shaking his head. "Having said that, there was a minor incident that occurred here this past Monday."

"Tell me more about it."

"Two men wearing military uniforms entered the market. They were handing out tracts to customers and shopkeepers throughout the market. When the men made their way to me, I noticed shoulder patches on their uniforms, featuring the French flag and the letters 'OAS,' each embroidered on each color of the flag. They handed me a tract, which I took."

"Do you still have the tract in your possession?" Karim inquired.

"No, I tossed it in the trash bin. It wasn't worth me keeping."

"What did it say?"

Ahmed shrugged. "Just OAS propaganda, about how Algeria will remain French, de Gaulle and the government cannot be trusted, blah, blah, blah. I'm sure you've heard it all before."

"Indeed."

"But that wasn't all. Not long after, both men raised their fists, and began chanting '*L'Algérie est française et le restera!*' Some of the patrons seemed to find the men to be a nuisance, although I don't think they took exception to the motto being chanted. Ultimately, the patrons succeeded in driving these two men out of the market."

"Were you in fear?"

"I was scared, as you can imagine, because I didn't know if they were armed and would thus launch an attack."

"It seems unavoidable, inevitable rather, that bloodshed will tear this city apart. I know it," Karim said. "Whenever I stop by, can I trust you as a friend, to keep me informed on whatever you see or hear regarding the OAS?"

"You can count on me," Ahmed replied, reaching out for a handshake.

We need to counter this, Karim said to himself. Someway, somehow. The propaganda war by the OAS was in full force, shaping public opinion within the city. Having the right tools at the FLN's disposal was crucial for them to respond likewise. The right man to turn to could only be none other than Yassine, the Minister of Information. Karim retrieved a 10-franc note that was tucked under his mattress before leaving home and, upon leaving the Casbah, employed the services of a chauffeur once again. The chauffeur drove through the heart of the neighborhood of El-Biar, passing by the cluster of palm trees situated at the central square, adjacent to the main street that was Avenue Georges Clemenceau where one could see Halal and European butcher shops within close distance of each other. A suburb that had its own charm, but wasn't any more immune to the conflict that was concentrated in central Algiers. The chauffeur dropped off Karim, who paid him with the 10-franc note, on Avenue Carnot at a quarter to three o'clock in the afternoon. Karim then walked to an address that served as a clandestine office for organizing various affairs within the FLN. Located on the second floor, there were no signs nor displays that indicated the nature of the business that was conducted at this address. A black curtain over the windows concealed the interior as well. Karim knocked on the door, soon answered by a woman. It was Zineb, the secretary.

"Come on in, Karim," she said, closing and locking the door upon his entry. Zineb, in her late twenties, slender, was wearing a checkered blouse tucked under a knee-length black skirt. Her black hair was rather short–just past the earlobes, and parted on both sides. The walls were void of any posters, bulletins, notes and the like. On one hand, it kind of gave the feel as if a new tenant had moved in recently. Yet, there was certainly no lack of office furniture nor equipment on hand with the desks, chairs, filing cabinets and typewriters. Zineb then went to her seat behind the desk, which lay a rusty typewriter. A fair amount of chipped paint marred a number of keys on it. It appeared that Zineb was in the middle of typing some kind of correspondence.

"I'm here to speak to Yassine," Karim said.

"He just left a short while ago, but he will be back soon."

"I'll stick around for now."

"I don't mind. In fact, I welcome the company. I'm just finishing typing up this letter which I have to drop off at the post office by the end of the business day. It will be going to Blida."

Resting on an office chair at the other end was a stack of papers. Karim moved to the chair and picked up a sheet of paper. "*L'APPEL AU PEUPLE*" read the title. *The call to the people.* A FLN document without question, he examined it further. "Did you type this or Yassine?" Karim asked Zineb, looking at her and holding the paper up.

Zineb paused her typing and looked up, meeting his eyes. "Not me. That would be Yassine's work."

Karim nodded his head and took a seat at a chair adjacent to the desk. Zineb resumed typing a few minutes more before pausing once again. She rose from her seat, and caught his attention. "There's something I want to show you over there," she said, motioning to the rear of the office. Zineb led him to a small filing cabinet, no more than about three feet in height, featuring two drawers. Its contents were secure, as evidenced by the keyhole. Inserting the key and opening the top drawer, Zineb pulled out tracts, many of them, all bound together with a rubber band. "Now these here, I was working on, especially with writing the inscriptions and composing the draft, as well as Yassine," Zineb stated, handing them to him. "Take a look."

Karim drew a tract out from being bound by the rubber band. The big, bold letters at the top jumped out at him as if a decree had just been proclaimed: "*À BAS LE FASCISME! À BAS L'OAS! REJOIGNEZ-NOUS DANS NOTRE LUTTE POUR UNE ALGÉRIE INDÉPENDANTE.*" Down with fascism! Down with the OAS! Join us in our fight for an independent Algeria.

Below the inscription featured the Algerian flag with both Europeans and Algerians behind it.

"Have copies of these already been distributed?" he asked her.

"No," Zineb replied. "Not to my knowledge."

"This is gold. These can be put for a useful purpose." Karim went back to take a seat, Zineb doing the same behind the desk. Minutes later, Yassine opened the door, only to look behind his shoulder and then take a glance around, before finally locking the door, enough to cause Karim to inquire. "Someone following you?" he asked him.

"No. At least I don't think so," Yassine replied. "It's just that I was assaulted on the street three days ago in broad daylight, so I'm on the lookout for anything that seems suspicious."

"The hooligans are becoming more and more brazen. Fucking scumbags they are!"

"An OAS sympathizer."

"I wouldn't expect anything less from one. But at least you escaped it unscathed."

Zineb excused herself to go pick up her five-year-old daughter from school, and then onwards for a run to the post office.

Karim looked around. "The discreetness of this place, I admire what you've done here," he said.

"We had to. If any French authorities stop by, even if God forbid it's a raid, to inquire about the nature of business we're conducting here, I'll just simply claim that we repair office equipment."

"The presence of the typewriter is a dead giveaway."

"And the disassembled electric pencil sharpener too," Yassine said, pointing to the parts in pieces to his left. "It gives the impression that we do not pose a threat, at least on the surface, if one were to look around here."

"Plus the notion that we operate a business and are contributing to the economy."

Karim rose from his seat. "I want to ask you about these tracts," he said, moving to retrieve them at the corner of the desk.

"Oh, those," Yassine replied. "...we only have a limited number of them because I was on the fence in regards to wanting to print and even distribute them in the first place."

"Any reason why?"

"Our efforts and resources should be exerted more towards diplomatic relations rather than the average, everyday citizen."

"Understood."

"But I must say though, the inscription does hold true to our message."

"May I take some of these?"

Yassine shrugged. "Sure." He then added, "but just be careful, be vigilant, around you and wherever you distribute them, should you decide to do so."

Yassine sat on a chair behind his desk, kicked his feet on top of it, leaned back and let out a loud yawn. He looked exhausted. "Lately I've been pulling in 12-hour days here at the office, much more than usual."

"And it's taken a toll on you?" Karim replied.

"Has it ever. Coordinating one FLN activity after another, preparing and publicizing press releases and other written material. Clandestine meetings with subordinates."

"It's all for a just cause. Something to always keep in mind, not that you've lost sight of that or anything."

"My wife has been complaining about me not spending enough time with the family; how the children need me, and so on. I always reassure her, and she seems to accept it, as far as I can tell."

"You owe it to yourself and them to spend a whole day or two with the family, and no one else."

"Which I will tomorrow, perhaps even the weekend too." Yassine made himself comfy in his chair, as if he was ready to take a nap. "Say, I have another matter to discuss with you, but let's save that for another time. I've been thinking of getting away from the city for a day, on Monday. It would be much appreciated if you can join me."

"Sure. Where do you have in mind?"

"Chenoua. A beach *escapade* for the day."

"I'll be there."

Karim picked up the hint that it was best to depart the scene, and leave Yassine alone to rest. So he did, leaving in the same manner in which he came.

Later that day at night, Karim sought to carry out the task he had been planning on for hours. Sporting the usual navy blue cardigan and slacks, he left home in the Casbah at nine-thirty sharp on a rather chilly spring night, on his way to Bab-el-Oued. Strapped over his shoulder was the messenger bag which contained the tracts. Traveling on foot, Karim soon made it to La Place des Trois Horloges, where a tall post was situated, featuring three clocks at the top.

He glanced down at his wrist. The watch read two minutes before ten o'clock at night. Not one person was in sight, so it was time to act quick. In distributing the tracts, Karim would have to go about it in a stealth way. On the Rue des Moulins, Karim began by slipping a tract under the door of a butcher shop, and later doing the same at a nearby *quincaillerie*, a hardware store. He spotted a random passerby; a pedestrian here and there–nothing, or no one to be alarmed of. A cold, crisp breeze permeated the air, bringing a shiver to Karim, causing him to tug at his sweater.

Onwards, Karim came to the Place Lelièvre, where a number of benches were situated at the square. He set several tracts on the bench seats, and then moved onto the Saint-Joseph Church. At the double front doors, Karim reached into his messenger bag, retrieving more tracts, and inserted them through the opening between the double doors. His work was done for the night, without being seen in the act as far as he knew, and Karim walked back home under the moonlight.

May 22. Parked on the Avenue du 8 Novembre at a quarter to ten in the morning, Yassine idled in his car, a sky blue BMW 326, until Karim arrived. They were off to the beach in Chenoua, west of Algiers. Days prior, with Yassine's approval, Karim was quick to invite Sebastián and his wife Claudia, both of whom could be of benefit to Yassine and

Karim. The two Spaniards were to take their own transport and arrive at the beach later in the day.

During the drive, Yassine shared how his aide, Akram, was fatally attacked on his way home the other day. Afterwards, chitchat ensued between Yassine and Karim, primarily regarding family matters. Upon arrival at Chenoua, Yassine hauled a large duffel bag and knapsack, with Karim helping out in carrying beach chairs as well as tall wooden staffs, which were to be used as poles in setting up a makeshift canopy. When they descended on the shore at eleven o'clock, it was almost void of beachgoers at this hour, although both knew that would change soon. The sandy beach and the still blue sea in front of them, with the coastal hills nearby. Above, clear skies, along with the blazing heat provided the perfect beach weather. Both trod through the sand in flip flops and soon found a nice spot to settle. They wasted no time in assembling the makeshift canopy. Inside the duffel bag, Yassine retrieved a navy blue bed sheet for the canopy's overhead.

"This should suffice, for four people; a nice shield from the sun," Yassine said.

"Let's not count on it only being four," Karim replied.

"You're expecting more to join us?"

"With Sebastián, you never know. He seems to be acquainted with every prominent figure in town–the type who will go the extra mile to lend a hand–and a man who is sympathetic to our cause."

"The more support we can get, the merrier. We can never have enough of it." Yassine rolled out a clean towel on the sand while Karim reached for a beach chair that lay next to the knapsack and unfolded it, taking a seat. Yassine continued, "Listen, we'll be organizing and launching demonstrations and protests, throughout the city, against these brutal attacks recently on Muslims by the OAS. With the help of others, of course, so we won't be alone."

The "we" was a dead giveaway; the inclusion left Karim convinced that there was no vagueness nor ambiguity in the intent of Yassine's comment. He conjured up a reply. "So I should take this as an invitation to get involved, *hein?*"

"I wouldn't be speaking to you today otherwise. Hey, if this'll be your first time entering the fray of protests, that's all the more reason for you to take part in it."

Karim thought about the involvement as a whole and what it would entail. "The opposition, the counter-protesters I guess you can better put it, will be huge."

"That is to be expected. It's already the norm."

"Two weeks ago, a local shopkeeper shared with me an incident at the Marché de la Lyre instigated by some OAS scum. Just imagine if dozens of us–"

"More like hundreds, we're anticipating," Yassine interjected, cutting him off, emphasizing the potential magnitude of the involvement.

"Just imagine all of us out protesting, what kind of reaction it will draw from the OAS...the chaos, the havoc."

"Well, it's not the time for us to be consumed in any kind of defeatist or pessimistic attitude. If that's the case, we'll wind up being ruled by the French for another one hundred years, as far as I'm concerned. And look, the OAS is desperately clinging on to a French Algeria whose future will be short-lived, so let's acknowledge that reality, and face this battle head on."

"Well said."

While waiting for the others to arrive, Karim reached into his beach bag and pulled out a book–the Albert Camus novel *L'Étranger*–picking up where he last left off to help pass the time. He only made it through five pages when Sebastián and Claudia finally arrived, sporting their *maillot de bains*, carrying a cooler and a picnic basket. Taking the initiative as was usual of him, Sebastián was quick to introduce himself to Yassine. After the exchange of compliments, Yassine downed a can of soda and excused himself to take a dip in the sea.

"Busy day at the office?" Karim asked Sebastián.

"It always is. My receptionist is handling all messages and inquiries in my absence," he answered.

Karim grinned, amused at another thought. "Isn't it something that, in the midst of a war, we're lounging on a beach as though there's no hint of any social or political turmoil taking place in Algeria?"

Sebastián nodded, "Well, you certainly chose the right place to be that feeds that impression."

"How much longer will this last?"

"Ah, the million-dollar question...But I'll throw in my guess here: If the war lasts beyond twelve months from now, I'd be shocked. French Algeria's days are numbered."

"That's more or less the same thing Yassine said."

"Although I just met him, from what I can sense, he's fighting the good fight, and you are too—and should."

Claudia meanwhile reached for a bottle of sunscreen and began rubbing her legs and thighs with a layer of sunscreen, and on up to her arms and face.

"Sebastián, there's something I've been meaning to ask you that's been sitting on my mind for a while now: Being that you're of European descent, why are you pro-FLN? How does an Algerian nationalist movement benefit you, a so-called '*pied-noir*?' It leaves me confused, to be frank," Karim inquired.

"Well, young man, I'll explain it to you," Sebastián replied. He reclined in the beach chair before continuing, "I was born in Bab-el-Oued. I spent my youth living in both Algeria and Spain. Throughout my young adult life, I was brainwashed into believing that we of European stock were superior to that of North Africans, and also sub-Saharan Africans. As Jules Ferry once said, 'It is our right, our duty, to civilize the inferior races.' This type of dogma instilled in me is what I came to believe. But, sometime in my mid-forties, I came to terms with the reality that we of European descent were the invaders, the exploiters, of the Algerians."

"I bet it wasn't easy coming to that realization."

"Not when you've been indoctrinated," Sebastián replied, a shake of his head.

"Did you come from a privileged background?" Karim sought to clarify his question, "Economically, I mean."

"Hardly. My father was employed at the Carrières Jaubert as a laborer for some forty years, doing the hard, back-breaking labor of digging and excavating stones, rocks, and other raw resources. Back in his day, that kind of work was dominated by us Spaniards. And my mother was a housewife, hence we lived in a one-income household. Thus, I strived to be the first one in the family to pursue a white-collar career; to earn a more affluent income than that of my father, and I succeeded. And so, in more recent years, I started using my position and influence in aiding the embattled in Algeria; those seeking justice. And I haven't stopped since."

"You've lived a meaningful life, and have made quite an impact."

"I'm 62 years old. Regardless of this war's outcome– Algerian independence or the prolongation of French colonial rule–I will be retiring in Spain in a few years. It's where my wife and I trace our roots to. We own a beachfront condominium in Alicante and we will live out our retirement there."

Claudia opened the lid of the picnic basket and after taking a demi baguette, she turned to Karim and chimed in, "Spain will always be home to us."

"And all this time I thought that you had something material to gain from being on the side of the FLN," Karim said.

"Far from it, my friend," Sebastián said. "You have a lot to gain from it, but not me."

A knife in hand, Claudia butterflied the baguette on the mini wooden coffee table that rested on the sand. "I can offer you a *merguez* sandwich; *merguez* straight from the butcher today and fully cooked," she said to Karim.

"Yes, that would be a delight. I'll take one," he replied.

"I also have *jambon beurre*, but I'm sure you won't take it."

"As a Muslim, I'll have to pass on that." An abstention from any cut of meat from a pig.

Claudia was quick to reach back into the picnic basket for the spicy sausage, adding sliced tomatoes and chopped parsley to the sandwich as a finishing touch before handing it to him.

Yassine returned and joined the others in having lunch under the canopy. Afterwards, Claudia and Sebastián took their turn for a swim in the sea. The beach crowd grew in numbers as the day carried into the early afternoon. As expected, the Europeans, basking under the sun. Yassine and Karim had set up the canopy far from the pedestrian footpath to the sand for more privacy, away from any beachgoer who may inadvertently overhear any conversation of theirs. Yassine reached into the knapsack to retrieve an item, which turned out to be a leather padfolio. Opening it, a sheet of paper was inside.

"Here. Take the time to study this. It's a press release I drafted, announcing our intentions to initiate a protest. Let's see what a bright, educated young man such as yourself can make out of this; any inaccuracies you may spot or any suggestions. As I mentioned in the car, my aide who was responsible for this is no longer around, hence I'm turning to you. Be my proofreader, if you will. As you know, I'm a bit more proficient in Arabic than French, and the press release is obviously in French," Yassine said, handing the letter to him.

Karim could not help but to feel that he was sitting in a classroom once more, but this time in nearly triple-digit heat outside. On the flip side, he saw that this brief evaluation of a written document might lead to something greater for him, in the near future, within the ranks of the FLN or elsewhere. He thus took the task seriously. The letterhead was succinct, and only one line: "FRONT DE LIBÉRATION NATIONALE." No address beneath it, nor anything to indicate a locale nor physical location where the FLN was conducting operations from. As for the content below, it struck Karim as simply a speech in written form that fittingly suited one occupied in the public relations field; nothing more, nothing less, in outlining the details of the FLN's intentions and motives for a protest to the press. Moreover, the clarity of the writing in terms of grammar and vocabulary was outstanding. "The content sounds fine to me, and the writing is superb," he said.

"Redactions won't be necessary then," Yassine replied.

"I'll join you for the demonstrations and protests. Count me in."

"Good. That's the response I was expecting anyway.

But with my aide no longer around, I'd like for you to also join me on the day of the scheduled press conference. Do know that you won't be in front of the camera. Unless there's a change of mind."

"Understood. But I wish to make my presence known, and felt, even if it is at a distance, so to speak. Little by little."

Karim handed the press release back to Yassine and rose from the beach chair to join Sebastián and Claudia swimming in the sea. Bathing in the turquoise blue waters brought a respite from the grind; the rigors of tumultuous Algiers. In more than one way, Chenoua was like its own nation, far beyond Algeria's borders, Karim said to himself. Sebastián and Claudia returned to the sand, yet Karim stuck around for a while longer, soaking up the sunshine and plunging himself underwater. When he left the water and rejoined the others, Sebastián pulled him over for a talk. "I've got something for you. Here's your ID, a counterfeit driver's license," he said.

Karim took it from him and brought the ID up close, near his eyes, analyzing it.

"You're listed as 24 years of age," Sebastián added.

"Splendid. This will serve its purpose. For now, at least, until I turn eighteen in the summer when I'd be eligible to apply for a *legitimate* driver's license. But moreover, I can now drive with more peace of mind, knowing I won't go to prison for driving unlicensed," Karim remarked.

"Moreover, you can now legally enter bars and night-clubs, if you so desire." Sebastián grinned.

A mere chuckle by Karim. "At some point, my assignments may entail undercover work where I will have to enter such an establishment."

A favor granted to him, Karim knew he had a good

friend at his side, one whom he was confident would be invaluable moving forward.

June 1. The Hôtel Saint-George was a palatial accommodation in the Mustapha Supérieur neighborhood. Designed in the Moorish architectural style, the hotel also featured a vast botanical garden and a huge swimming pool, among other amenities. Palm trees were abundant throughout the property. Beyond its interior and exterior beauty, the hotel was a playground for prominent as well as rich visitors–celebrities and wealthy businessmen, especially English. In addition, military brass frequented the place, most notably the U.S. military. A place where these prominent visitors would find exquisite dining, and as such, wine and dine their guests, carry on a fling with a person they had met there or with a significant other.

Located at 24 Avenue Foureau-Lamy, the proprietor of the hotel was a wealthy English businessman by the name of Alfred Caruthers. Or, *Sir* Alfred Caruthers, as he preferred to be called. Much of his wealth was attributed to sports betting, and, later on, he pursued investments in film finance companies, as well as the acquisition of actors' and playwrights' studios in London. In a failed attempt to purchase the Hôtel Aletti from the famed Joseph Aletti, Caruthers succeeded in the purchase of the Hôtel Saint-George in expanding his real estate empire. Caruthers, well into his seventies, chubby, north of six-feet tall, had a full scruffy beard as white as snow. Glen Moray Scotch Whiskey was his alcoholic beverage of choice. A man who once suffered a stroke, yet survived, was instantly recognized by the pince-nez glasses he wore.

Yassine arrived, and sat on a bench in the botanical

garden, surrounded by a plethora of trees. A dirt walkway led towards the hotel's entrance and he was certain that Karim wouldn't encounter any difficulty in locating him. Once Karim made it on scene, Yassine led him to the outdoor dining patio in showing him around the property first. Chic Europeans enjoying a brunch under the sun, engaging in pleasant conversation without a care in the world, as if political and war-time turmoil didn't exist. A stop by the pool followed, and then onto the interior of the hotel. It struck Karim right away as to why the hotel attracted the prominent and wealthy. Exquisitely designed and decorated Moorish architecture, from arches connecting to its columns in the main dining hall to Iznik tiles adorning some of the walls.

At the enormous dining hall, some twenty or so tables were present, although only a handful of guests were dining. A menu was resting on top of one of the unoccupied tables. Karim picked it up to glance at the food selection. Yassine moved around, apparently looking for someone in particular. In viewing the menu, among the high-end selections that were notable: Sole meunière, royal shrimp, codfish aioli, veal cutlet, while also featuring cheeses such as Camembert and Roquefort.

Yassine returned to Karim, who was still viewing the menu. "Wow, the food offerings here sound so appetizing," Karim said.

"Pricey, isn't it?" Yassine responded.

"You've got that right."

"I haven't much of an appetite."

Karim seemed a bit bummed by that remark. "Well then that settles it, because I certainly won't be dining alone."

"We're here for business, and I can't find the man I'm looking for. Just stay put for now."

Karim did so, and Yassine moved around again, only to return a minute later, accompanied by a sharp-dressed man in a gray suit, with a black tie, lean and tall, sporting sunglasses. "Follow me," Yassine said to Karim. The men soon entered a reception room, and instantly, an overwhelming, nervous feeling consumed Karim in seeing the vast members of the media and cameras in the room. Rows of chairs occupied much of the room, and a stage with a long rectangular banquet table was to his right where the primary speakers would be seated. Karim took a seat on a chair at the far corner of the room, well away from the shots of the cameras. The press conference commenced right away, no delays whatsoever. Karim sat there, listening to the speech with intrigue and interest, one that was uninterrupted and given by Yassine, in which he read off his press release, announcing the FLN intentions to initiate protests in Algiers. The speech lasted around the five-to-ten-minute range.

Shortly after, Yassine descended from the stage, Karim rising from his seat to join Yassine. They were then approached by a young French man, accompanied by two other men beside him, who looked to be the camera crew.

"*Bonjour*, my name is Antoine. I'm a journalist with Le Monde. I would like to conduct an interview with you, if you don't mind," the journalist politely asked.

Yassine seemed to be slightly annoyed at the request. *Really? You had to ask me this?* "I just conducted a so-called interview. Was that not enough?" he answered.

"Well, sir, with all due respect, that was more of a speech, not an interview. Please, I just have some questions to ask regarding the goals and objectives of your organization, or movement that is, the FLN. Nothing more than that."

Yassine was adamant that he'd only agree to do so

under a condition that he set forth. "I'm not going to do it in front of a camera."

"No problem, that's fine with me. All that I will have on hand is my notepad and pen."

"Fair enough. But before doing so, I'm going to have my associate here search you and your men to check that you're not carrying any sort of weapons."

"Sure, by all means."

Yassine turned to face Karim, and motioned to him. Karim went ahead and did *la fouille*, the up-and-down body search on Antoine and his two camera crew men, certain that they carried no weapons whatsoever. "All right, let's proceed," Yassine said.

"There's another reception room down the hall. Let's go there. We'll have more privacy," Antoine said.

Antoine led the way. He was a young Frenchman, surely in his twenties, sporting a gray suit and slacks, lean, a clean-shaven boyish face, and rather long, wavy blond hair that was neatly combed. A handsome man, in fact. Indeed, he came across as a vain man, in terms of appearance. They entered another reception room, featuring round banquet tables draped with white tablecloths. The room was pretty much the same in size as the other they had been in earlier. Antoine, Yassine and Karim took a seat at a table while the two camera crew men, having set their camera equipment aside, not to be used as per the condition set forth by Yassine, sat at another.

Antoine set his notepad on the table and, pen between his thumb and index finger, he moved his chair a bit closer to the table, ready to get the interview underway. "As I'm sure you know, and I'm not trying to be critical, nor even discredit the FLN's efforts and vision here, but for Algerian independence to become a reality, serious diplomatic discussions between both sides have to gain traction. So, in the interim, what are the FLN's more immediate goals and objectives?"

Yassine looked at him, surprised at the question. *Isn't it obvious?* "To exercise our will, and force the de Gaulle-led government to engage in serious diplomatic dialogue with us, by any means necessary. One, as you heard, by initiating protests in the city, and elsewhere. Also, to strike fear into the European community that we are a force to be reckoned with. And in addition, getting nations to join us and ally with our cause. We won't give in until all of our desires are fulfilled."

Antoine nodded his head. "I see. Understood," he said, jotting down notes on his pad.

"We're at war, and not enough people around the world are talking about it. This should be considered a humanitarian crisis, and the fact that it isn't being treated as such is reprehensible."

"Well, American President Kennedy has voiced support for your cause."

"And God bless him. But his support is not enough; we need much more."

"Well yes, of course," Antoine replied. "Now in regards to communism, and with the FLN engaging in dialogue with Communist regimes such as China and the Soviet Union, does that not make your movement–"

Irate, Yassine cut him off. "All we care about is our own destiny. Not that of others. I couldn't care less how Khrushchev or Mao run their own countries."

"But you're still–"

Yassine cut Antoine off again. "They've welcomed us, and have been willing to listen to us. And with that, joining us in taking our cause to the international stage. They're willing to aid us if need be."

"So that's not to say that you embrace Communism or its values?"

Yassine scoffed. "We, the FLN, we are not a Communist organization, nor hold Communistic ideals. In fact, I equate Communism as the polar opposite to our values and beliefs."

The interview came to a conclusion, with Antoine thanking both Yassine and Karim for their time. Walking out of the reception room, Yassine turned to Karim, saying, "Well, come to think of it, the only good thing to come out of that interview is that you were present, and to witness and listen to this firsthand. May this experience open your eyes to the mindset of the other side. If it doesn't, then I don't know what will."

Karim shook his head. "Man, I'm glad the interview didn't last long and truth be told, I was kind of hoping it would abruptly be cut short. I mean...*wow*. I guess that monosyllable best describes it."

"They're always portraying us as the aggressors, the perpetrators, the troublemakers."

Karim sought to invite others, as many as he could, to participate in the upcoming demonstrations and protests. *Algerians only?*, so the question arose, though in reality, it didn't really matter if those who agreed to join were Europeans, or even Jews, so long as they stood in support with the FLN. Back to driving an automobile again, Karim rented a BMW for a couple of days. He was in the neighborhood of Belcourt. Cruising down the congested Rue de Lyon, he soon turned onto the Rue Fontaine Bleue and headed uphill, amidst yet another day of heat bearing down. The *bidonville*, shantytown, of Cité Mahieddine was nearby, but well away from the main road.

Passing by an auto shop, Karim continued until nearing an electronics store when he spotted a gathering to his right that caught his attention. About a dozen men, most with their backs leaning against a wall, congregating as if they were waiting to be solicited for employment. Karim pulled over to the right and parked the car. Almost immediately, four young men approached the vehicle.

Karim leaned towards the passenger's door, window fully rolled down, to talk to the men. "What can I do for you guys? In need of any help?"

"We're in need of work," one of the young men replied, succinct.

Karim shook his head. "Sorry, friend. I can't help you there."

"Please, we beg of you, sir. Not only for ourselves, but to put food on the table to feed our families. I've three children, and they often go hungry."

A statement that Karim felt bummed about, because it was something that he could relate to in coming from a poor family. "Don't know what else to say. Sorry. I'm no employer. I'm here actually to invite those who'd like to join and participate in the upcoming FLN protests in town. Would you men be interested?"

"What's in it for *us*?" he replied, a sort of entitled remark.

Frozen, at a loss for words, Karim was looking for the correct response to give, in large part because it became quite apparent that giving an answer along the lines of 'voicing our demands for justice, equality, and sovereignty' was not one that the man was looking for. He finally uttered, "Nothing tangible, I can say."

The man, along with the three others beside him, turned around and walked away without saying another word. Feeling sympathy for the men, Karim sincerely wanted to find a way to help them somehow. He leaned back in his seat and let out a deep sigh. Out of nowhere, in what seemed more like an epiphany, he recalled his encounter with Lila, one of the cooks for the ALN, and the food shortages they had to deal with. Like planting a seed, this gave him an idea, a very bold one to say the least, that he could suggest to the men. *That's it!*, Karim thought.

Not a moment to waste, Karim acted quick to share the plan he had in mind and honked the horn a few times to get their attention. He then got out of the car. "Hold on!" he shouted. The four men turned around. "Come over here!" Karim shouted again, also gesturing with his hand.

They approached the vehicle once more, meeting Karim. To not have some random passerby inadvertently overhear the conversation by chance, he ordered the men to get inside the car. Once in, Karim continued, "Say, a thought just crossed my mind. Call me crazy if you will, but here it goes: How about we break into a farmhouse and rob it, pillage it of its food supplies? Let's seize as much as we can."

The same man who had been speaking to Karim, seated in the passenger's seat, thought about the suggestion for a moment. He then responded, "Well yes. Let's do it. I'm all for it."

"Good deal then. We're in agreement. We'll leave here tonight."

"But man, I must say, this is going to be dangerous."

"*That* it may be, and I'm not trying to downplay it at all, but aren't we already living our lives in danger?"

"You're right. I cannot disagree with you."

"Still being colonized is worse." Karim glanced at his watch. It was only four-thirty in the afternoon, too early to leave town as his plan was to strike at night. He looked to his right to face the man. "We're going to need some equipment and such—masks, knives, a heavy-duty wrench and screwdriver—and whatever else we can think of."

"Me and the other guys will get whatever we can find."

"Likewise. Let's meet here at eight o'clock this evening."

The man agreed, before giving his name—Mehdi. He, as well as his three companions crammed in the backseat, got out of the car and left, to return in the evening.

A few hours later, nightfall had already set in, and Karim returned to the scene and idled in his car. Given the difficulty he had earlier in finding a nearby hardware store, he should have just asked Mehdi about it. Instead, Karim finally found one as a result of asking a pedestrian. At any rate, he had walked out of the hardware store with a wrench and screwdriver—to remove the car's license plates to make the car unidentifiable—as well as a knife and duct tape.

Karim glanced at his watch. There was no sign of Mehdi, nor the others who had accompanied him. Out and about were a minimal number of men smoking cigarettes, surely catching some fresh air during this warm evening.

He continued to wait. It was now ten minutes after eight in the evening. Karim was nervous, worried, wondering if the men had second thoughts about joining him and were no longer interested. No more than three minutes later, lo and behold, Mehdi and three men beside him arrived.

"Man, you had me worried. I thought maybe you had a change of heart," Karim admitted.

"Seeing what we potentially have to gain, we're not going to pass on this," Mehdi replied. He had a large brown sack in hand, identical to a potato sack.

"Let's get in the car and we'll talk."

Once the men were inside, Mehdi revealed the sack's contents. "This is what I brought: Rope and head scarves to be used to conceal our faces." Karim gave a quick look at the goods. "I searched for balaclavas, but no luck finding them," Mehdi added.

"These will do just fine. Let's not waste any more time and get going." Right away, they hit the road.

The nighttime drive led Karim to take it easy and slow, not so much that he would encounter another roadblock, but rather the slight fear that he could get pulled over for possibly speeding, among other things. Moreover, to avoid possibly taking the wrong road as a result of a lack of visibility of the highway signs.

"So where to?" Mehdi asked him.

"South of here, to the Mitidja, in the direction of Blida."

"I figured so."

"It will be at least a one-hour drive from here. I'm looking to take the same route as the last time I headed out there, and for good reason. But the thing is, I wasn't doing the driving then–it was a chauffeur."

"What made you think of this?"

"This is just between us, OK?"

Mehdi nodded, further agreeing with a simple "understood."

"On a recent visit to the Aurès mountains, I came into

contact with a cook for the ALN. She proceeded to tell me about the food supply shortages within the army, and the impacts of it. I've told myself since, 'I wish to be able to help her, someday soon.' So, out of nowhere to be frank, after you walked away from my car, the story this woman shared with me seemed to have struck me like an epiphany, and that was when I proposed this plan to you," Karim said.

"Wow, you've been around and have done a lot, it seems. Even more so for a young guy like yourself. And way out in the Aurès, no less. I myself have never been there."

"Then, and even now, I sympathize with her story. So, if our plan tonight turns out successful, and I fully do realize that is a big *if*, I will do my part to provide her with much-needed food supplies for our soldiers."

"Yes, indeed. But what makes you think that we'll find what we're looking for? And plenty of food supplies, that is."

"There must be, because I remember the chauffeur pointing in one particular direction and telling me that there was a *silo*, which I was completely ignorant of its meaning at the time–a word I had never even heard of before. When I inquired about it, he went on to explain what it was, as well as inform me of the farms in the vicinity. As if that wasn't enough, he also gave me the lowdown on the French farmers in the area, the foods they specialize in harvesting, the vineyards and so on. Clearly a man who has a great deal of familiarity with the landscape and the local economy in the area."

"All I can say is, you seem confident about going ahead with this, as if you know what you're doing."

"I'm no stranger to being a thief."

In the latter part of the drive, Karim turned on the

high-beam headlights for increased visibility. It was now half-past nine o'clock at night and he pulled off the main road, immediately turning off the headlights once he spotted the silo. The farmhouse in question was on the other side, and perhaps one-fifth of a kilometer away, all the while, the car was treading lightly, no more than 20 kilometers per hour. To make their efforts get off on the right foot, Karim parked the car under an Algerian oak tree, the ideal spot for the car to be unseen from the dwellers of the farmhouse, which was a few hundred yards from the tree.

The men got out of the car in unison, as quietly as possible. On second thought, Karim opted not to remove the license plates from the car. It was unnecessary, he told himself, given the darkness of the night and the car not being parked too close to the house. He also reminded, or rather emphasized to the others, to avoid lethal violence at all possible; to only exercise the adequate force needed to subdue the occupants inside. Sitting on the dirt ground, backs leaning against the right side of the vehicle, each man put on and adjusted the head scarves appropriately, a secure concealment of the face. Each man also tucked a knife into their back pockets while Mehdi put the roll of duct tape into the other back pocket.

A single-story house with a clay-shingled roof, it was also long, basically rectangular in shape at its base. Monitoring the house to determine which way to break in, the men would peep over the car and then duck their heads from time to time in an effort to avoid being seen. A light was on inside the house, which appeared to be from a lamp in the living room area. The men idled patiently, waiting for the right sign or moment to make a move. At least a half an hour had passed, and one of the home's occupants opened the back door and left it partially open, surely to allow fresh air to circulate inside the house on a warm night. The opened back door was their sign to spring into action. Karim whispered to his accomplices that he would give the nod to make the move within moments. When he did so, the men quietly rose from sitting on the ground and approached the rear of the house with caution. Karim guessed that no more than three or four people occupied the house at best, giving him confidence in succeeding in this crime. The men now leaned against the back wall of the house, only feet away from the back door. Karim gestured to the men and he then led the way, entering the premises, one step at a time.

The sound of a man and a woman engaging in chatter could be heard within earshot. Treading down the small corridor, Karim came to a halt. Ahead of him was a desk, partly illuminated by light that had to come from a lamp. The living or dining room of the house had to be to the right, Karim thought, since not one person was in sight. He peeked past the edge of the wall, and spotted a man sitting on a *fauteuil*, an armchair, as well as a woman sitting on a sofa, adjacent to the man. The chatter between the man and woman carried on, and Karim, giving a thumbs up to the accomplices lined up behind him, made the bold move and dashed towards the man! The elderly man came to see that Karim was charging at him, and quickly reached for what looked to be a knife on the side table. The woman on the sofa let out a desperate plea of a scream. By the time the man could reach for the object, Karim met him with a back-hand blow of his fist, meanwhile Mehdi and the two accomplices delivered a blow to the woman's face and pinned her to the floor. Karim wrestled the man to the floor and managed to strike him once more in the head, injuring him. He now had this man pinned to the floor and subdued. He held onto the man by his neck, waiting for the accomplices to tie the woman's hands behind her back with duct tape. Karim then did the same to the man.

"Food supplies? Where are the food supplies?" Mehdi asked the woman.

The woman was still perturbed by fear and the shock of being clubbed in the face; the realization of the breaking and entering. No answer from her. "*Répondez-moi!*" Mehdi said, with a hint of anger. *Answer me!*

She seemed to struggle with being able to vocalize, but finally let out a reply. "There's a storehouse. Outside."

Mehdi brought the woman to her feet, his right hand grasping the back of her neck. Meanwhile, Karim also bound the man's hands with rope for good measure.

"Show me where it is," Mehdi demanded, and he led the woman out the front door.

Karim followed suit. "On your feet!" he said to the subdued man. "Don't utter one word unless told otherwise." Gripping the man's shirt from the back collar, Karim led him in heading out the front door. They came to the others who were standing in front of the storehouse, which resembled a shed. One could see the numerous nails that were embedded into the sturdy wooden door, secured by a brass padlock.

"Where's the key?" Karim asked the man.

"In my right pocket," he replied.

"Don't move." Karim reached for it, pulling out a plethora of keys on the ring, which he happened to fumble and drop, but picked up right off the ground. "Which one?"

"The one painted green."

Karim wasted no time in unlocking the door. He opened it all the way and Mehdi turned on the flashlight, handing it to him. Karim was the first to step inside, shining the light all around. Three barrels of what surely had to be wine were the first items he saw. A shovel, as well as various tools were present, and then Karim spotted what he and the accomplices had sought: Sacks and sacks of grains. Large, full ones. Several dozen kilos, perhaps more. Karim then turned to the captured man. "What do we have in here?"

"Barley, millet, flour, couscous."

"Splendid!" Karim could not have been more pleased. "Khalil, pull the car up here," he said to one of the accomplices. Karim tossed the car key to him, and, in the meantime, continued to examine the storehouse.

The sound of the tires treading on the dirt ground increasing ever louder, it soon came to a stop. Khalil popped the trunk open. The home's occupants, hands still bound by duct tape, stood helplessly by, without saying one word as ordered, watched their property being robbed in front of their very own eyes. All five men loaded the car with the goods, making several trips back and forth until the food supplies were all taken.

"Bring both of them in here," Karim said. Mehdi and Khalil led the two occupants inside the storehouse. Karim shut the door, then inserting the padlock into the hasp and closing it, effectively locking the man and woman in the storehouse. "Let's get the hell out of here!" he then said.

The men dashed into the car, and within moments Karim sped off, back onto the highway. Karim undid the headscarf. "That wasn't so bad, was it?" he remarked.

"Not at all, in fact. We pulled it off, and without inflicting brutal violence upon them," Mehdi replied.

"Just as I was hoping for."

Mehdi turned to Karim to give him a high five.

"With the heavy load we have in the trunk, I don't want to be driving fast," Karim commented.

"The trunk is stuffed to the brim. Take it easy behind the wheel. Don't be in a rush to get back to Algiers."

"Well, your family will love what you have in store for them when you get back home."

"It's all thanks to you. None of it would have otherwise been possible. I must tell you, Karim, your boldness, courageousness, is remarkable. Inspiring to me, if I may say."

"I'm flattered, really. But all of this is about something much more, much greater than just me. You understand what I mean, right?"

Mehdi was quick to nod his head, agreeing. "It is well understood. I'm sure you may have taken my response the wrong way about asking me to join you in the protests, but you can rest assured I will be there."

"Glad to hear it."

The men arrived back in Algiers on Rue Fontaine Bleue just minutes before midnight. Mehdi directed Karim to his residence, just around the corner. Karim reminded him, "I'm afraid you'll only be able to take a limited number of food supplies from the trunk. I made a commitment that I will deliver food supplies to the ALN and I refuse to back away from that commitment."

"Yes, that's fine with me," Mehdi replied. "But you're not leaving right after dropping me off, are you?"

The question left Karim a bit bemused in what was obvious to him. "Of course, I am. What other choice is there?"

"My dear friend, please spend the night at my place. It's almost midnight, you shouldn't be driving around any longer."

"Home is not far away from here. It won't take me long to get there."

Mehdi seemed a little disappointed. "Are you sure?"

"Certain."

The car was parked on a dirt road amidst the slum that was the Cité Mahieddine, and Karim turned off the car's lights. "Only three sacks, nothing more," he told the men. "That's more than enough to keep you guys, and even some of your neighbors, going for a while." They unloaded the car, as quietly as possible, and transported the goods into one of the dwellings that was a shack. The noise from the shuffling of feet on the ground while carrying the sacks woke up a few neighbors. As soon as the task was complete, Karim closed the trunk and drove off, heading home, the repeated yawning a sign that it was time for him to get some rest. The long haul to the eastern part of the country to deliver the food supplies to the army would be saved for another time.

Several weeks had passed. As the season drew towards the latter part of summer, the mood of the city's inhabitants, the Algérois, was filled with anger. Skirmishes and riots broke out between the FLN and the OAS, as well as their sympathizers, during the demonstrations and protests that took place throughout the city. To make matters worse for the FLN, word broke out that de Gaulle was contemplating a 'partition' of Algeria, whereby the European population would carve out their own separate enclave. To which, not surprisingly, the FLN, enraged, took to the streets to voice their opposition. In the FLN's view, it was a proposal that effectively said: *even if Algerian independence is granted, not all of Algeria will be ceded to the Algerian people.*

More than just the ever-mounting turmoil between the FLN and OAS, there was something else that brought concern to Karim. On a phone call of no more than three minutes long with Sofiane, Karim sensed in the tone of Sofiane's voice that he sounded pessimistic and defeated; disheartened. But he flat out refused to state why. It was abnormal and totally unlike him, Karim thought. *Was a major blow dealt to the FLN on foreign soil? Was Karim about to be dismissed from his duties in the FLN? Or, had the frequent overseas travel finally taken its toll on Sofiane?* As for Sofiane abruptly ending the phone call, Karim wondered as to the phone call possibly being tapped. Questions arose, but Karim couldn't get any answers until Sofiane returned to Algiers.

The days slipped by, into the final week of August. Out of the blue, on a sunny Tuesday around nine o'clock in the morning, Karim was alarmed by a loud knock on the door. Being alone at home, he proceeded to the door in slow steps as the knocking continued, fearing that perhaps the police traced him in a manhunt for the suspects involved in the *L'Écho d'Alger* bombing. Opening the door with caution, ever so slightly just to peek and see who it was, he then exhaled, relieved.

"Oh, it's you, Sofiane. You're back!" Karim uttered.

"With me, you never know," Sofiane replied.

"Well, you've come at the right time because no one else is here." Karim opened the door all the way and Sofiane entered the apartment.

"I had to ask three passerbys how to find the street here."

"I figured so. If the French authorities have trouble navigating these maze-like streets, just imagine how it is for the average visitor."

The aroma of roasted eggplant still permeated the tiny living room space. "So what's new? Did something go terribly wrong?" Karim then asked.

"Our demands were not met, so the talks ended in failure." Sofiane shook his head in disgust.

"I see. A huge disappointment. That must have been a waste of time on your part. All that can be done is to persist; here on our soil, I mean."

"I hate taking 'no' for an answer." Sofiane moved closer to the dining table where some *kesra* and a jar of sour cherry jam lay, as well as a plate of leftover roasted eggplant slices. "May I?" he politely asked.

"Help yourself."

"There's also been a shakeup within the FLN leadership. I will now be serving as the Minister of Finance and Economic Affairs."

"Wow, really? That's a nice title to have," Karim remarked. "But in your view, do you see this as good or bad, compared to your previous role?"

"I would say that I was comfy in my role as the Minister of Foreign Affairs, but sometimes change is needed, and that can be a good thing. But otherwise, I feel kind of indifferent about it."

"Sounds like you're doing what is needed and in the best interest of the organization."

Sofiane finished consuming a mouthful of bread and a piece of the roasted eggplant broken off with his fingers and then said, "Remember our meeting in Sebastián's office when he mentioned about a lawyer in Paris?"

"Yes, I do recall."

"Karim, I now ask you for a favor; two in fact–your next assignment to better put it: I want you to go Paris and meet the lawyer. Work with him on how to best go about moving funds from Paris to us here in Algiers. We need it now more than ever."

"Paris?" Karim uttered in astonishment, met with a nod by Sofiane. "Uh, wait, I will be able to board a flight, right? Should I–"

"Oh," Sofiane said, cutting him off, and then reached into his inside jacket pocket, pulling out an ID–a national identity card. He handed it to Karim. "Problem solved."

Karim examined the contents, focusing on the name and age shown.

"I put you down as 23 years of age," Sofiane added.

Karim read the name. "André Vasseur."

"I figured a French surname will draw less suspicion. It will give the authorities the impression that you come from a French father."

"You know, I have a phony ID that was given to me by Sebastián?"

"May I see it?"

"Sure." Karim reached into his wallet and pulled out the ID. "I hadn't thought of it a moment ago," he added, handing it to him.

Sofiane took a good look at it. "For one, *this* ID here is a driver's license. Secondly, it has your true legal name. Use the ID that *I am* giving you, a national identity card, which has you listed under an alias. Trust me, you'll be better off by operating under a name that is not your real name when engaging in clandestine activity in Europe."

"Understood," Karim replied. "But Paris? Wow, I always thought I'd someday pay a visit there."

"There's glamour to be seen and experienced, no doubt. But the thrill of it wears off after a while. Take my word for it, I've been to Paris a number of times."

"And the other task?"

"There's a manhunt for a FLN fugitive in Paris. He's been fighting the good fight for us, longer than you have, and on French soil, no less. I want you to assist, and help execute his escape out of the country."

"All by myself? In a land I have no familiarity with?"

"Here's my instruction to you: Your first point of contact is with the lawyer. His name is Sami Bekkouche. Establish rapport with him. I am confident that he will put you in contact with the right people–those who are FLN allies."

"FLN allies in France? Surely they're few and far between."

"Believe it or not, the numbers are greater than what one may assume. There's even French men and women who sympathize with the FLN, who would otherwise be viewed as turncoats by their compatriots. They just operate 'underground,' so to speak." Sofiane pressed on, "Can you catch a flight tomorrow morning?"

Karim took a seat at the dining table, as if to buy himself time to answer. "If you really need me to go, then I'll do it."

"I'll take that as a *yes*. Tomorrow morning it is."

"For how long?"

Sofiane shrugged. "Two weeks or so. Or when the job gets done."

"Fair enough then. I'll let my mother and siblings know that I'll be leaving town. Upon arriving in Paris, what will be the first order of business?"

"First and foremost, check into a hotel. I have written instructions inside a large envelope that will tell you everything you need to do. Just follow them–they're pretty straightforward. We'll review the instructions together before arriving at the Maison Blanche airport tomorrow.

I want to make sure you don't leave town with any unanswered questions."

"I'll need money to sustain myself during my stay."

Sofiane pulled out his wallet from the back pocket. "I've got you covered." He counted the bills, one by one, of what were many. "Here's 1,600 francs. That should sustain you for a couple of weeks, perhaps more, even in an expensive city like Paris. I expect you'll splurge somewhat, but don't overdo it."

The clean, crisp bills in the palm of his hand, Karim had never held anywhere near this amount of cash in his possession. It was not appropriate to simply stare at them, so he folded the bills and tucked them in his front pants pocket. "I'll start packing. But first, I'll need to go buy a suitcase. You'll be giving me a ride to the airport in the morning, right?"

"Of course."

Karim let out a sigh. "May God be with me."

III

The airplane touched down at Orly airport outside Paris at midday, arriving on a terrain which Karim considered to be a foreign land, though in reality, both the metropole and Algeria were governed by the Fifth Republic. The phony ID worked to perfection, sparing Karim, operating under the alias of André, from encountering the run-around and possible interrogation as to the intent and purpose of his stay. Clearing this hurdle, André was more assured of his getting around without issues.

He caught a taxi and was on his way to the center of town to take care of the first order of business, which was to check into a hotel. Per Sofiane's order, André was to avoid staying at a pension. The sensitive documents he carried, coupled with the lack of privacy by having possibly several other guests around was a bad idea. The privacy of a hotel room on the other hand, save for the daily cleaning done by the housekeeper, was the most suitable option. The taxi traveled along the Boulevard Périphérique and in due time, arrived at the Hôtel Gérando in the 9th arrondissement. A reasonably-priced hotel dating back to the 1920s, it was situated close to the center of the Right Bank, well away from the fringes of the periphery.

The check-in was less than smooth, however, as the hotel's female front desk clerk eyed André in a way that left him a bit uncomfortable, giving a look of appraisal on a few occasions. *What business do you have being here?* was the sense André picked up by her expression. André couldn't tell though if she was actually looking at him in disdain or signaling a sense of attraction. At any rate, it wasn't enough to deter André from walking out the door and finding another hotel to lodge at. A closer look at the woman's name tag above her left breast revealed Clotilde. Her demeanor seemed to change once André pulled out a wad of bills from his front pocket and opted to pay for the room for the entire week instead of by the day. *Money talks.*

Finally entering his room on the second floor, André found it to be an elegant, dream-like place. A fully fur-nished room featuring a king-sized bed–and one with a mattress on a bed frame, unlike the mattress he slept on back home–as well as a television, both items foreign to him at his place of residence. Moreover, the room featured a balcony, overlooking Rue Gérando. A far cry from home, and not one person to turn to nor trust in the capital city of the colonial enemy. *At least not yet...*

September 1. André left the hotel in the mid-morning hour, allowing enough time to arrive before the scheduled eleven o'clock appointment with Sami Bekkouche at the Duvauchelle & Giraud law firm. A *boulangerie* was located just down the street and André quickly grabbed a *pain au chocolat* and an espresso for breakfast, something he wouldn't bother having back home. Clean shaven, sporting casual business attire with his usual navy blue cardigan, André sought to present the image to Monsieur Bekkouche that he was someone to conduct business with. Yet, he felt ill at ease, jittery to better put it, in meeting some stranger in a land far from home, even more so given that there was no prior contact initiated between the two–no phone call, no correspondence–just a meeting that was arranged.

André opted to pay for a taxi to the law firm located on Avenue de Wagram, in the 17th arrondissement, as he was not familiar with public transport in the city. When he got out of the taxi, he held his head up and brushed off the concerns lingering in his head. After passing through the entrance, he informed the receptionist of his appointment and patiently waited, taking a seat in the lobby. There was a delay in Sami's arrival, but when he did descend from upstairs, André instantly picked up the grace of a man who was refined, walked with confidence, assured of himself; a man who embodied success–at least from the outside. Sami wore a pinstriped double-breasted suit, vest underneath, slacks, and was lean, tall and well-groomed; an Algerian man who was around his late thirties.

"You must be André?" Sami said.

"Indeed I am," André replied, reaching out for a hand-shake, Sami reciprocating.

"Follow me upstairs to my office."

The inside of Sami's office was immaculately clean, simple, conservative, albeit the furniture was more on the older side, including the two bergère chairs. Wall hangings were minimal. Once both men were seated, desk between the two, Sami studied André closely, almost squinting.

"You look younger than I imagined," he said.

"Being young plays to my advantage in this line of work, slipping through the cracks, and having had many escapes like Ali la Pointe."

"God forbid you share the same fate as him." He offered André coffee, who politely declined. Sami then reached for the pack of Gitanes cigarettes resting on the desk, sliding one out and lighting it. He exhaled a puff of smoke and met André's eyes. "You can tell me your real name. I know that you've been sent by Sofiane. We're on the same side here."

"Karim," André replied. "But please, I've been advised that it's imperative that I go by an alias here in France, and it's best that I follow the orders of my boss."

"Oh certainly. It is well understood. I just had to ask." Reclining back in his plush office chair, Sami asked, "Even though I know already, let me hear, in your own words, the purpose as to why you've come to see me."

"Well, it's two-fold. First, I've been assigned to help a FLN fugitive escape Paris and ultimately out of the country. Second, as you know, my other mission is to acquire funds to send or transport to Algeria to be used in our ongoing war effort; funds that can be used not only for firearms purchases, but to further our social, economic and political agenda. These OAS fucks continue to pose a greater and greater threat, and, dare I say it, they appear to be well organized."

Sami changed his posture from leaning back to sitting in a more upright position. "As for helping a FLN fugitive escape Paris, I think I know who you're referring to. Is it Ibrahim?"

André nodded his head, "Yes, that's him."

"I figured so. I can imagine him being crucified by the press, and perhaps even the general public, if he gets caught. Do you know anything about him and what his deal is?"

"I know basically nothing about him. As you can guess, I'm not attuned to what goes on here in Paris, other than the bits of information I hear from my inner circle."

"Well, in a nutshell, dozens of Algerian laborers were severely beaten by the police. As far I see it, it was for no reason other than the crime of being Algerian. So, in a reprisal, Ibrahim bombed a metro station near the Canal Saint-Martin. There's been a manhunt for him ever since."

Thinking about his own recent experiences back home, André remarked, "Sounds familiar. Something I can relate to."

"Huh? What do you mean?"

"Ah, never mind. Go on."

"But the problem is, he could be hiding out anywhere in the banlieues, if he is even in the Paris region at all. Were you given any hints or clues of his whereabouts?"

"Yes, in fact. I was given a street address."

Sami nearly jumped out of his seat. "No kidding? Do you have it with you?"

"It's in my wallet."

"Allow me to take a look."

André pulled out the folded note in his wallet, handing it to him.

"Ah, Argenteuil. Looks legit to me," Sami said.

"It has to be legit; this came from Sofiane."

"Yes, of course." Sami pulled out a pen and a notepad and made a note of the address. "Don't act on this just yet. Allow me some time before I advise you the plan to take from here."

"Understood."

"Now, as for the other favor you're asking, here's what you need to know: It has become more and more difficult to smuggle funds out of France, be it across the border, or to North Africa. There has been a tremendous crackdown by the authorities in lieu of the whole Jeanson Network collapse. Are you in the know of what I'm speaking of?"

André shrugged. "Somewhat, I suppose."

"No doubt, it has made the headlines here. Don't know if it has in Algeria."

"From what I hear, Mr. Jeanson seemed to have succeeded. Well, at least for some time, anyway."

"Well, to his credit, he had an extensive network of cohorts at his side—political allies, intellectuals, and so on." Sami stubbed out his cigarette in an ashtray. "Illegal financial activity has been deterred and people think twice about committing it. Don't get me wrong, illegal activity is still going on—there's no denying that. The exchange of funds between Algerian workers and the FLN does happen 'under the table,' so to speak. But please know, this is not intended to discourage you, nor even say it is impossible to achieve, I just want you to understand the reality of what to face. To be able to transport funds out of France and to Algeria, it's going to be a tough task to successfully pull this off."

"I value your input, and I don't doubt that it is correct. But, I didn't come out here for nothing." André looked him right in the eyes.

"Meaning?"

"It's a risk worth taking."

Sami nodded, taking the cue that André didn't, or wouldn't accept leaving France and returning to Algeria empty-handed in what André would consider a failed mission. "One more thing I need to make clear, and it's not for me to be the bearer of bad news, but my help to you would be limited in capacity. You see, I am a member of the Paris Bar, and I cannot engage in conduct, or actions to better put it, that would put my professional reputation on the line, lest I be stripped of my position and have no recourse but to return to Algeria. I've had the fortune of establishing relationships with medium and even high-ranking Parisian officials, and I cannot risk possibly losing my livelihood here in Paris due to engaging in criminal activity. Please know though, and I tell you this with all sincerity: My heart is and always will be with Algeria," Sami said.

"Understood, and I would never suggest that you put your career or livelihood in jeopardy. I just ask that you put me in contact with the right people who can help me in my mission. Surely you know someone."

Sami steepled his hands, soon arriving at a response that would please André. "You're in luck. I know the right person to contact." He leaned forward a bit, continuing, "But first, please join me this Monday. I will be in the outskirts of town meeting up with men involved in the overseeing and managing of the funds collected from Algerian workers. You can kind of think of it as union dues. Who knows, we may even stop by on-site where the Algerian laborers are employed. See firsthand what really takes place behind the scenes with these funds, and, ultimately, engaging in the scheme of smuggling the funds out of the country. Consider it a mandatory appearance for someone like you who's a complete novice to this type of activity."

"I'll be there. You can count on me."

"Meet me here first thing Monday morning–nine o' clock, the time that we lawyers start business for the day, and we'll depart immediately thereafter." Sami reached into one of the desk drawers. "Where are you staying at?"

"At a hotel in the 9th arrondissement."

"Do me a favor. Try to keep a low profile during your stay. Don't say much to strangers. Be mindful of who you attempt to befriend. Try to avoid large gatherings."

"That's been my mindset all along."

"I tell you all of this for good reason. Anyone suspected of being an Algerian can and does get accosted and inter-rogated by the *flics*, and I've even seen it happen by your ordinary Parisian on the streets. In short, it's for your own safety."

"I appreciate the heads up."

He felt intimidated to a certain degree. Above all perhaps, André chalked up his encounter with Sami as a *teenager meets adult* kind of talk. Unlike Sofiane, whom André found immediate favor with, that was not such the case with Sami. André was convinced that he simply hadn't earned the trust of Sami–yet. He arrived at the law firm before the scheduled meeting time of nine o'clock in the morning, once again waiting for Sami to show up.

Sami descended on scene, and led André out the door. "The car is down the street," he said. Both men made a stop at a nearby *boulangerie* to have some *viennoiseries* and coffee for breakfast before making it to the car, a cream-col-ored Renault 4CV. Once inside, they took off right away.

"Help me out here with this, André," Sami began, "Sofiane sent you here to help a FLN fugitive escape, not to mention smuggling funds out of the country, knowing full well that there are pro-FLN operatives, including French ones mind you, who have succeeded with these assignments. Yet he still sent you here to carry out this mission? Is there something I'm missing here?"

"Nope. Nothing you're missing. He wants me to take up this challenge in the metropole; to flex my muscles as a dangerous operative, so to speak; to see what I'm made of."

"And did you have any reservations about this at first, or did you just jump on it with enthusiasm and decided to go all in?"

"I had my reservations at first, and hesitated, upon hearing that it meant I would have to go to Paris, a place far away and one I had never set foot in. Once I agreed to go to Paris, I decided to go 'all in' as you put it, and embrace the challenge."

"Hmm, something tells me he might be doing this to test you, to see if you can pass, possibly grooming you for a higher position within the FLN in the near future."

André, who was somewhat slouched, now sat up in a more upright position, absorbing what he had just heard. "You know, I've thought of that before. And now, hearing it from you as well, there really must be something to it. Perhaps the time has come for me to not just see myself solely as a subordinate type."

Sami slammed on his brakes at a stoplight on the Boulevard Berthier, amidst the heavy auto and pedestrian traffic, though he didn't appear to be agitated by it at all. Parisian women passing along the crosswalks and sidewalks in their stylish dresses, even on a gray summer morning; men in their business suits, a number of them moving in an apparent rush. "Don't underestimate yourself, André. Think ahead to the future, and what a nationalist Algerian government will look like in a free, independent Algeria? And I believe that day is coming sooner rather than later."

"Point well taken."

"When native, pure-blooded Frenchmen, and women, are sympathizing and aiding our cause, that should be a telltale sign that the clock is ticking for colonialism in Algeria."

Out of the confines of the Paris city limits, past the periphery, the men were now approaching the suburb of Colombes. The surroundings by sight were much a work in progress. Beyond the existing housing structures, building projects abound.

"Modern housing," André remarked.

"Take a wild guess who these are for," Sami replied.

"Algerians?"

"Yep. One can only stay living in a hotel or pension for so long. Or heck, even the *bidonvilles* for that matter."

"You don't think these would be suitable for the penniless French students?"

"Well yeah, I would have to say so. But they are not the primary intended recipients." Sami slowed down, looking around, but didn't appear to be lost. "The bigger question is, after independence is gained, how many Algerian workers will return to Algeria, and how many will stay in France due to the lure of earning higher wages here?"

"For those of us active in the pro-nationalist movement, that is a question that should concern all of us."

"These days, people will sell their identity and soul for the almighty dollar."

André shook his head, disgusted. "Shameful."

"For me, I could easily afford to rent an apartment in one of the more ritzy arrondissements, a stone's throw away from the Eiffel Tower, but choose instead to live in a modest studio, north in the 18th, closer to where you find an Algerian presence. I don't envision myself being here in France very long. It's not home to me."

"I don't blame you for feeling that way."

In thinking of the address that they'd be heading to

later, Sami remarked, "But speaking of Ibrahim, it's no surprise to me, based on the information you had provided me, that he's not hiding out in a *bidonville*. See, you have to think like a criminal and know where it would be ground zero for a manhunt and avoid it."

"Tell me more about the *bidonvilles* out here."

Sami shrugged. "What's there to say? I mean, a slum is a slum, you know? I wouldn't advise you to go to one; not in Nanterre nor elsewhere; really because there's no reason for you to."

"I was at a *bidonville* earlier in the summer in Algiers. No harm done, no sorts of dangers seen."

"Well that's good. Out here though, if a sharp, young stranger like you ventures into one, you can be seen as having some kind of ulterior motive for being there. Just my opinion."

They were now clearly in a construction zone, away from the center of town. A small building past a scaffolded, unfinished edifice appeared to catch Sami's attention, where two men stood outside, chatting with each other. Moments later, Sami pulled over and parked the car. He revealed to André that the building was in fact an office building and that the business in the front was operated by a man who worked as a self-employed architect. Sami went on to mention that their meeting with the overseers and managers of the funds was to be in a "rented office space" in the rear of the building. The self-employed architect, Laurent, who sympathized with the FLN, was paid "a fee" for his service in allowing the men to utilize the rear office space within his business' premises.

Sami and André got out of the car and headed towards the building, in the direction of the two strangers. After being greeted by both men, Sami introduced André to them. The first man, a Frenchman named Thierry Menard, surely in his fifties, dressed professionally, sported a flattop haircut, salt and pepper stubble on his face and wore horn-rimmed glasses. To André, Thierry gave off this air of being a principal at a distinguished school in his appearance and persona. It turned out that Thierry was actually the owner of a construction business and one that managed numerous building projects in the environs, as well as employing hundreds of Algerians.

The other man, who went by the name of Youcef Taleb, claimed to be the Chief of Wilaya 2 for the French Federation of the FLN. In the same age range as Thierry, Youcef on the other hand was an Algerian, had a bald head, as well as being clean shaven on the face. The checkered blazer coat he wore stood out above all. Small talk among all the men ensued to break the ice and establish rapport.

Sami turned to André and said in a soft voice, "André, I'm going to have a word with the men in private, just hang tight out here."

André nodded his head and Sami, along with Thierry and Youcef, went to the back of the building. In the meantime, rather than simply idle by the car, André meandered down the street to kill time. Within minutes, he sat down on the curb. He knew exactly what Sami's purpose in engaging in discussions behind closed doors was all about; no need to even inquire. The sound of trucks, chainsaws and other machinery in operation was loud, but still bearable, as a throng of laborers were hard at work building some structure farther down the street.

Several minutes passed, and André rose from sitting on the curb. Shortly after, a whistle was heard, followed by a shout. "André!" It was from Sami, and he called out

André's name more than once, also gesturing by hand. André went straight to Sami.

"You're going to be pleased with the news you're about to hear, *and see*," he said.

Sami led him to the rear of the building and into the office space. Filing cabinets were situated against a wall across from the door. Two large wooden tables placed side-by-side lay smack in the middle of the room. On one table was a sky blue suitcase, opened, carrying a boatload of cash. Youcef was standing next to it while at the other end of the table was Thierry.

"Can you be trusted with this amount of cash?" Youcef jokingly remarked at André, a wide grin on his face, and chuckled.

"I've yet to disappoint anyone on the job," André replied, letting out a short laugh.

"Come here," Youcef said. He grabbed a wad of bills and handed it to André. "Get a feel for this kind of cash," he added.

André took the wad in his hand. At a glance, the notes were a mix of crumpled, crisp and soiled bills. Scanning his eyes at the other bills inside the suitcase, they all looked to be in the same condition. "Splendid. Fucking splendid!" he uttered.

"André, we came to an agreement to arrange a hefty sum of cash to be smuggled out of the country, and eventually direct to Sofiane," Sami said.

"It will be much to his delight, and mine too. Once the accomplices, the vehicle and logistics are settled, I'll be on the move once again."

"There will be more than what you see here. Money from other contributors will be added on Friday, at which point you can then leave Paris with the dough and smuggle it into West Germany," Youcef stated.

"Fantastic," André replied.

Thierry jumped in, adding, "The Controller will run a tally on the total amount, but rest assured it is in the millions of francs."

"So everything here stays with you for now?"

"Correct. You'll need to pick it up here on Friday."

A *fait accompli* as far as André was concerned. He felt satisfied in fulfilling this duty, and above all, he had cohorts assisting him along the way. Leaving the office, it was now onward to the next task.

Back in the Renault, they took off once more en route to Argenteuil, another suburb located only a few kilometers away. Crossing the Seine via a bridge, Pont de Bezons, Sami soon arrived at the address with little difficulty, pulling over and parking the car. Fingering the folded note out of his front pants pocket, André studied it once more to ensure that they arrived at the right place. The address indicated an apartment dwelling; a building structure about fifteen stories tall.

"Shall I accompany you?" Sami asked André.

"Nah, I'll take care of this. I know you've gone out of your way in helping me thus far, and the truth is, this is my business to handle," André replied.

"Are you sure?"

"Yeah."

"If anything happens; any kind of danger you may encounter, please head right back here."

"Understood. Nevertheless, I need to make every effort to find this man."

André exited the car, with Sami staying inside. To André's delight, there was no 'checkpoint' to clear, no guards to be searched by, as was the case back home in Algiers' Casbah. Heck, not even any fencing nor gate surrounding the complex; it was just walk to the front double-doors and enter the building. The elevator took him to the eighth floor and on to unit number 810, just as the address on the note indicated.

At the door, André gave a few rather gentle knocks. There was no answer, so he gave a few more firm knocks the second time around. Still no answer, he gave it one more go, a third round of knocking on the door. This time, someone answered–a pale-skinned, middle-aged woman whose head was covered with a headscarf.

"*Puis-je vous aider?*" she asked. *Can I help you?* There was not a hint of any accent in her voice whatsoever. Moreover, judging by her face, André found that this woman did not have any Algerian-looking features. He was positive that she was a French woman.

"Yes, madame. My name is André and I am here to see Ibrahim," he answered.

"What for? What brings you here to see him?"

"I've been sent by my superior to offer help."

She was silent for several seconds before replying, "Is it just you alone?"

"Just me."

The woman, apparently not believing André, then peeked her head out the door and glanced down both ends of the corridor for reassurance.

"I've no reason to lie to you, madame," André said.

She hesitated, and looked him up and down, the look of appraisal, perhaps still skeptical. The woman finally gave in. "*Entrez,*" she said. *Come on in.*

André took soft steps in entering the apartment.

"Take off your shoes," she added, and André did so. "Come, this way to the living room." A rather plump woman who was dressed in all white, including her apron, she led him from the entrance towards the living room. Arriving just before it, to what was a hallway to the left, a man descended out of nowhere, armed with a hammer! The man raised the hammer, letting out a loud grunt of rage, in motion to strike André, before the woman jumped in, protecting André from being assaulted. "*Arrête*, Ibrahim! *Arrête!*" she yelled, pleading for him to stop.

Startled, in a panic, André backed off several steps and threw both hands up, as if surrendering to a *flic*. "I'm here to help! I come in peace!" André cried out. "I come in peace!" he repeated.

Ibrahim nearly barreled his way past the woman in an effort to get closer to André, clearly not convinced yet by André's appeal. The woman continued to obstruct by getting in Ibrahim's way, attempting to placate him.

"I'm an Algerian with the FLN. I'm here to help you!" André pleaded once more, but this time speaking in Arabic. Now speaking in a language that was a mother tongue to the typical Algerian, it appeared to placate Ibrahim.

"OK, all right. All right," Ibrahim finally yielded. Seconds later, he placed the hammer on a nearby stool. André's nerves diminished, slowly but surely, bringing himself at ease. Ibrahim continued, "I didn't mean to terrify you like this, but I suspected you were one of the authorities, or even one operating undercover."

"No worries, it's all understood. You've got to do what is necessary to defend and protect yourself," André replied.

"Please take a seat," he said, gesturing to one of the sofas. A coffee table lay right in the middle of a living room that was spotless. André sat down and made himself comfy, now feeling more at home. Ibrahim, over twice André's age, had a shaved head–cutting all his hair off to alter his appearance since becoming a fugitive–, wide shoulders, was even taller than André, and wore a casual white shirt, dark brown pants and black steel toe shoes.

"Huguette, please bring us some tea," Ibrahim called out, facing the woman. Turning back to André, he continued, "So, fill me in on what's your deal here in France?"

"Well, since it wasn't evident at first, I've been sent by Sofiane to help you in orchestrating an escape out of France."

"Ah, so you're the one?"

"Indeed I am."

"Allow me to welcome you, my friend. You've made it here and I'm glad to make your acquaintance. Tell me a bit about you."

"Well, in short: Algérois, high school dropout, joined the FLN. I've been traveling throughout Algeria carrying out missions in support of our cause."

"Hmm, sounds like you've built quite a résumé already."

"Don't know if you've heard about or are aware of it, but the bombing of L'Écho d'Alger, I was involved in it," André revealed, in a way of bragging about one of his accomplishments.

"I am aware of the bombing, Sofiane told me about it."

Huguette brought out a tray with the cups of tea, saucers underneath. It was a black tea that had to be the Turkish kind.

"Sounds like we have something in common; bombings, that is," Ibrahim said. "I've done the same in Paris."

"You acted alone?"

"Yes, I did. Why do you ask?"

"I figured so. You seem like the kind of man who flies solo, so to speak."

"I was convinced that doing so would make it easier for me to escape unharmed, which was the case. Unfortunately though, I didn't succeed in going unnoticed, and, well, here I find myself."

André took a sip of the piping hot tea that almost burned his tongue. He quickly set the tea back down on the coffee table. "You seem to have found a hideout here, and are out of harm's way."

"But even here, in a suburb, there's no doubt in my mind that the police have Argenteuil on their radar, since we are still in the Paris region after all, which is why I can't stay here much longer. I won't even bother to walk down the street due to fear that someone will recognize me. Thankfully, Huguette handles all of the grocery runs, so I stay put here in the apartment. But how much longer can I stay cooped up in this apartment? It's not good for my well-being, you know."

In a slight change of topic, André remarked, "I don't mean to pry, but is she your wife?"

Ibrahim pursed his lips, shaking his head. "Nope. Just a kind soul who has taken me into her home. I am indebted to her."

"God bless her."

"Even so, my time here is reaching an end."

"And your intention is to head to Algeria?"

"Absolutely. Back home to Oran. Even when it was suggested to me to stay in France and find employment by using an alias and disguising myself, I said no. It's too much of a risk for me. I am a wanted man, and if I get caught, there will be no mercy upon me. And the fact that I committed an act of terror in the heart of the capital doesn't help matters for me either. I need to get out of France first and foremost, and then figure out how to get to Algeria."

"As I understand it, I will be off to West Germany in a few days. That's where I go after leaving Paris."

"Suits me fine. What day?"

"Friday."

"Four days from now? OK, that works for me."

"I'm sorry, I don't mean to cut this short and abruptly end our conversation, but my associate is waiting for me in the car."

"No worries, André. By all means."

André rose from the sofa and was led to the door. Ibrahim shook his hand.

"André, I'll be expecting you soon."

"I'll be back."

September 6. The day brought unpleasant weather–gloomy, gray clouds and skies–over Paris on a Wednesday morning. The sprinkles here and there picked up to a moderate rain by the late morning. Nevertheless, André owed it to himself to take some time to enjoy the City of Lights and hit the streets to visit its iconic landmarks: ascending the Eiffel Tower–his mind was blown away by the astonishing view of the landscape–, followed by a visit to the Louvre museum, a stroll on the Rue de Rivoli, and then to the Champs Élysées. Parisian men riding down the tree-lined street in bicycles with a Gitanes cigarette between the lips; women wearing long pea coats and high-heels, seated at a café terrace sipping on an espresso. For André, indulging in a succulent *steak au poivre* bathed in a rich green peppercorn sauce, followed by a decadent, smooth, silky *mousse au*

chocolat satisfied him immensely. That afternoon, prom-
enading through the Arc de Triomphe, André carried the
swagger of a young foreign prince strolling into a capital
city, without a care in the world.

In the evening, André was getting ready to meet two FLN
sympathizers, as advised to him by Sami the day before.
Though not a vain man by any means, he spent a few extra
minutes grooming himself well, before heading out the door
of the hotel. The heart of the Pigalle district, famed for its
nightlife, was a short walk away. It was one thing passing
by in the daytime, *but* at night, it was a totally different
animal. Beyond just the bars and nightclubs, there were
the cabarets–its flashing neon lights enticing one to walk
through the doors, be it a sin indulger, or even an innocent soul 'exploring' the area. André recalled Sami telling
him that *"anything goes"* with regards to the cabarets in
Pigalle, and that had to mean *pleasure*, and many sorts of
pleasure to be had, André imagined. He knew full well he
was stepping into a world he otherwise wouldn't bother
venturing in, but kept the perspective in mind that he was
out conducting business.

Moving on foot from Boulevard de Rochechouart
to Boulevard de Clichy, André arrived at his destination
within minutes. The meeting place was Cabaret Albin, its
sign illuminated with changing colors. Throngs of people
hobnobbed on the sidewalks outside other night venues.
At the entrance, André was met by a bouncer and handed
his phony ID. A smooth check-in. From the moment André
entered the cabaret, he was put off, almost repulsed, by the
ambiance of hedonistic pleasures from the patrons. Men
flirting with and even kissing women, who were elegantly

dressed. The cabaret music being played featured lyrics that at times were more on the naughty side. The sense of feeling ill-at-ease did not totally overwhelm him though. In spite of this, he had a job to do. André went straight to the bar and approached the first bartender he came across.

"I'm looking for a man by the name of Stéphane De Leneer," he said.

"That would be me. What can I do for you?" the man replied.

"Can we talk over here?" André asked, gesturing away from the bar.

"Sure." Both men moved towards the doorway that led to the restrooms, a good distance away from the dining area. Stéphane, a native Belgian in his late-fifties or so, had curly white hair, sported glasses, a small beer belly, and a black cardigan over a pinstriped shirt. He definitely came across as being 'the boss.'

"I've been sent to see you by a lawyer named Sami. I'm with the FLN."

"*Ah bon*? Good, you're one of them," Stéphane replied, sounding pleased to be of assistance.

"And I'm here two-fold: To get accomplices to join me in smuggling funds out of France, as well as smuggle a FLN fugitive out of the country."

"Understood. You've come to the right man. But first, I have to excuse myself for a short time, and then we can discuss the matter at hand. In the meantime, let me seat you. Follow me."

Stéphane led André to a window seat–a plush, velvet red booth seat in the dining area. "Can I get you a drink?"

"No, I'll pass," André answered, assuming all that was available were alcoholic drinks. He waited patiently for some ten minutes for Stéphane to return.

"Multitasking, as usual," Stéphane said. Now seated, he continued, "We need to be careful that our topic of discussion at hand isn't overheard by others. For obvious reasons."

"Given the volume of the music being played, we should be fine. Nevertheless, we should be mindful of others getting too close to us."

"You still haven't given me your name."

"Call me André."

"So, let's get down to business. When are you leaving Paris with the funds and to get the fugitive out of town?"

"Friday. That is the target date."

"*This* Friday, right?" Stéphane asked for confirmation.

"Yes."

He was a bit surprised by the short deadline. "Less than two days away? OK, I don't see that being a problem. I'm waiting for one of the accomplices. She should be joining us here any moment."

"*She?*" André uttered, caught off guard that a female would be involved, from the sound of it.

"Of course. She is a brilliant woman. Believe me, women serve a useful purpose in the underground FLN movement and have been successful at it."

"Well, if you say so, sir. I'm fine with it. I am not a sexist by any means."

"And which border are you looking to cross?"

"West Germany."

Stéphane raised his eyebrows, as if he was expecting a different answer or was not pleased with it. "Do know, I won't be the one driving you there."

"If I may ask, is there a reason why you can't? I mean, I realize you're busy with work, but if the lack of availability is not an issue, I'd be more than willing to compensate you handsomely for it."

"Sorry, André. As someone of Jewish descent, I have my objections on entering German soil, even with the country being split now. I'm sure you're understanding of that."

"That explains it succinctly."

Within moments, burlesque dancers descended on scene–on the small performing stage–dressed in their skimpy outfits, much of their bare flesh exposed. André, repulsed by this excessively-revealing display, all but had enough. "Oh no," he remarked.

"What is it?" Stéphane replied, baffled he appeared.

André rose from his seat and began to make his way out of the cabaret. "What is it?" Stéphane repeated.

"Look at this!" André replied, gesturing towards the women.

"What? The women?"

"Of course the women. What do you think I'm referring to?"

"This is harmless."

"Harmless? The women are half nude! I'm a Muslim. You should know that we consider this stuff, promiscuous sexual displays, as outright sin."

"They're not completely nude, at least. Secondly, they're only out on stage for a very brief time, and will be followed by cancan dancers, who are much more clothed. Just relax and stay calm."

"What do you mean by 'a brief time?'"

Stéphane gave a short shrug of the shoulders. "Fifteen minutes."

André grunted, and turned towards the exit. Stéphane caught up to him, and then put his left arm around André's shoulder to placate him. "André, my friend. Just relax and calm down," he repeated. A woman sporting a beige pea coat entered the cabaret and passed by, to Stéphane's right. "Look, I know a man who owns an auto shop in Aubervilliers, just north from here. In fact, he's the other accomplice. He'll be the driver, and he'll use his own car as the getaway vehicle to drive you and the others across the border into West Germany." Stéphane paused to let that sink in. "So what do you say?"

Hearing this, André realized that his mission would be a step closer to being fulfilled, and it was enough to persuade him to stay. He couldn't walk out now. "Well, that is what I came here for," he said. André shrugged his shoulders and said, "I'll stick around."

"*Ah, c'est ça, mon pote.* That's what I want to hear. Look, I will pay the man a visit at his auto shop tomorrow to inform him to depart on Friday. He's done unexpected jobs at the last minute, and I'm good friends with him, so I don't see any problem with him departing on Friday."

"Happy to hear it."

"C'mon, let's take a seat." The two men went back to the booth seat, only to find the same woman who had just passed them by a moment earlier seated there. "André, there's someone I want you to meet. She will accompany you when you leave town. Take the time to get to know each other," Stéphane said. He then excused himself and headed back towards the bar area. The woman, surely no older than forty, slender, wore a long, spaghetti strap black dress, had black hair parted on both sides, and bright red lipstick. A woman who could easily pass for a model.

"Pleased to know that someone will be joining me," André said.

"Likewise," the woman replied. "So I hear you're not from the region, is that right?"

"Correct. I am from *El-Djazair.*" he answered, noting the land of his residence in Arabic with purpose.

"Oh, my. And here you are in Paris. You're motivated, I can see. You're here with a sense of purpose."

"Determined, resolute. But I do as I'm told. And moreover, I've been advised what to look out for, what to expect, and how to carry myself during my time in Paris."

"You've been led on the right foot, it sounds. Half the battle is finding people whom you can trust in a city like Paris."

Stéphane brought a steaming pot of *moules marinières*, topped with chopped parsley and garlic, served with a basket of *frites* and garlic aioli on the side, along with a glass of red wine for the lady. In an act that surprised André, the woman patted the leather seat beside her, in a gesture for him to sit alongside her. "Come sit next to me," she said.

André did so without hesitation, while wondering if she was about to get flirty with him. "I think it's better this way. We can hear ourselves better," she added.

"So, what's your name?" André asked.

"Call me Mireille."

"Lovely name." He then wondered, *I'm not even going to ask if that's your real name.*

"*Merci.*"

"So as I understand it, you basically work underground for the FLN, right?"

"Yes, that's right." Mireille reached for a mussel, fully opening the shell with both thumbs and then snapping off the shell in half.

"So tell me, what are some of the jobs or missions you have carried out?"

"I've assisted the French Federation of the FLN with press and communications needs, delivered discreet packages to destinations not just within Paris and its environs, but outside the region as well. And other things too." Using the broken off empty half shell, she scooped out the mussel from the other half and inserted it into her mouth, taking several chews to fully digest it.

"Good. It helps me to get a better idea of who I'm dealing with, and to determine if there are any similarities to the work I have done."

"You're not going to eat any mussels?"

"I don't eat shellfish." Nevertheless, André reached for a few *frites* and dunked them in the garlic aioli as Mireille took a sip of the wine. He continued, "What motivated you to join our cause?"

"The mistreatment, abuse, and torture of Algerians."

"Have you witnessed this firsthand?"

"In Algeria?"

"Anywhere."

"To a degree, yes, I have in Paris. Admittedly, I've never set foot in Algeria."

André smiled and chuckled. "How rightful of you to state my homeland as Algeria, and *not* French Algeria."

"As it should be. Europeans do not belong there." Mireille reached for a *frite* and ate it. "A dear friend of mine, Dorothée, she has since returned home to Rouen. I don't know if '*missionary*' is the right word to use, but she went on an expedition to Algeria, out in the countryside, and she documented the extent of how the Algerian people have been disenfranchised, abused, killed, and denied equal rights on their own land. When she returned to the metropole, she was quick to share with me what she witnessed."

"Indeed. All of this I know too well."

"I am a staunch advocate and promoter of human

rights and justice. That's all the motivation I needed to ally myself with the FLN."

"This is much satisfying to know. It sure sounds to me like you're not in this to enrich yourself."

"*Pas du tout.* While I do get compensated of course for the missions I carry out, the pay is nothing to brag about. But hey, you've got to maintain a livelihood and put food on the table, you know."

"Certainly."

"And what are your intentions from here?"

André moved closer to her, put his right arm around her shoulder and whispered in her ear, "To help a FLN fugitive escape Paris, and smuggle him out of the country, as well as the smuggling of funds. It's where I lean on the help, and expertise of others, including you."

Mireille nodded her head, as if she'd done this before. "Yes, understood. That's why I'm here."

The cancan dancers descended on stage, ready to commence their performance. As Stéphane noted, their attire was not anywhere as revealing nor sexually inappropriate as the burlesque dancers. Otherwise, André excused himself to look for Stéphane. Once he found him, André called out his name.

"André, please don't tell me you have an issue with the cancan dancers," Stéphane remarked, grinning.

"No, no. On a more serious note though, I've got to ask this question: Can she be trusted? Mireille?"

"Most certainly. She's been thoroughly vetted by a FLN committee, and more than once, I might add."

"FLN committee?" André uttered.

"Yes. Besides, didn't Sami recommend her? I'm sure he wouldn't make an erroneous recommendation."

"Why yes, you're exactly right. I should have–" André

paused briefly. "I hadn't thought of that. It completely escaped my mind." He paused again, and resumed, "My mistake. I guess it's just the emotions, the feeling of doubts that crept in my mind."

"She's done this a number of times already, so don't think she's a novice."

"I guess I'm just looking for reassurance. I appreciate your input."

André returned to his seat. "Mireille, let's work together and set out what needs to be accomplished. Let's meet Friday morning in front of the Duvauchelle & Giraud law firm. From there, we'll be leaving town. You know where the law firm is, right?"

"Yes, I sure do."

"I imagine we'll be meeting very early, before the start of the business day. But first, stop by here tomorrow evening to confirm with Stéphane the exact hour we will meet. I will do the same. He will have coordinated the time, and logistics I suppose, with the auto shop owner by then."

"The earlier we leave, the better."

"Each of us will need to bring enough clothes and anything else needed to sustain us for a few days or so."

"Sounds good. See you then."

Two days later, partly cloudy skies hovered above Paris on a Friday morning at the crack of dawn, free from any precipitation. André was looking forward to meeting up with Mireille, largely due to the chemistry, so he sensed, between the two of them, that he was convinced would result in a successful collaboration. He left the hotel and when arriving at a quarter past six o'clock on Avenue de

Wagram where the law firm was located, Mireille was there waiting for him, as was Sami.

Right away, the three got into Sami's Renault and took off. The first order of business was to pick up the loot–the suitcases stuffed with bills–at the same office building in Colombes. On arrival, Sami stayed inside his vehicle as André and Mireille headed to the office space in the rear of the building. The two were greeted by Youcef and another man, who introduced himself as Walid Messaoudi, one of the Controllers for the French Federation of the FLN. Walid unveiled two large, durable sky blue suitcases, stuffed with notes. According to him, the tally came to a total just less than 2.5 million francs. Not wanting to waste any time, Youcef and André each carried a suitcase to Youcef's car–also a Renault, but a black one–and placed them in the trunk, as Youcef would be doing the driving from there. André then moved towards Sami's vehicle and gave Sami a 'thumbs up,' the signal for him to depart the scene as everything was all set and the entire loot was in good hands.

Onward, the next stop was to Ibrahim's hideout in Argenteuil to pick him up and carry out his escape from town. This time though, Mireille would accompany André to the apartment. After arriving, the two headed to the entrance and ascended the elevator to the eighth floor. Knocking on the door of unit 810, Huguette answered within seconds.

"Good morning, madame. Is Ibrahim here? We're ready to depart," André said.

"*Ah, oui, oui.* He'll be right out," Huguette replied.

In no more than a minute, Ibrahim appeared, sporting a gray-haired wig as a disguise.

"I'm back, just as promised," André said.

"I'm thankful you kept your word, my friend. I'm all set. Let's go," Ibrahim replied.

Mireille introduced herself and offered her pea coat to pull over Ibrahim's head as a means to conceal his face. Down the corridor and into the elevator, they made it to the ground floor in no time. Ibrahim tugged the collar of the coat over his head, Mireille walking arm-in-arm with him as if she was his lover. A smooth, albeit a sort of rushed walk back to the car. Engine on, Youcef hit the gas pedal and drove off. The mood inside the car was solemn, perhaps somewhat anxious, at least so until leaving the region entirely. Anything detrimental to their agenda was capable of occurring, so they all believed.

Some twenty minutes later, they arrived in Aubervilliers, another suburb situated just north of Paris. The auto shop was located on Rue de Valmy. The iron gate that secured the premises was open. Youcef pulled the vehicle into the driveway and parked. Mireille, Ibrahim and Youcef stayed inside the car, for now, allowing André to take the lead. He got out of the car and approached the garage. Inside, on the walls, featured auto parts of all sorts–struts, belts, and more–hanging on nails hammered into the walls. The tall shelves contained a plethora of motor oil bottles. At the far end of the garage, André found a man behind a desk, sitting on a short swivel stool, tinkering with an engine part using a wrench and a plier.

"*Bonjour*. You must be Guillaume?" André asked.

"Yes, I am. And you are?" he answered.

"André. Your dear friend Stéphane sent me. He tells me you're the best in the business at what you do."

Guillaume laughed. "Surely he didn't mean just my gig as an auto mechanic." He rose from his seat–a man decked in navy blue from shoulder to toe, surely in his sixties, both clean cut and shaven, with salt and pepper hair–and approached André. "Well, my services are in demand. Stéphane paid me a visit yesterday. It goes without saying, you're in need of my help to drive you across the border?"

"That's right."

"Well, I'll have you know, I've done this many times in the past year, to the point where I've become accustomed to it."

"Hey, I'll leave it all to you. You decide what route to take."

Youcef appeared, having left the vehicle. He was warmly greeted by Guillaume; two men already acquainted with each other, engaging in catch-up talk.

"Two more are sitting in the car and will be joining us," André pointed out to Guillaume.

Guillaume nodded his head. "Follow me." He led André through the side door and to another garage that was attached. A vehicle covered in tarp lay smack in the middle. Guillaume proceeded to open the shutter of the garage, yanking the chain with several motions, allowing natural light to penetrate inside. He then removed the tarp, which revealed a white Citroën Traction Avant that looked to be in pristine shape, both inside and out.

"Here she is. Solid, reliable, she gets the job done," Guillaume said.

"She's a beauty," André added.

With the car key in hand, Guillaume popped open the trunk's lid, and lifted the board, revealing the trunk's floor pan, eager to show something to André. "As you can see, the trunk's floor as well as the back seating have been tampered with, allowing more space for storage," Guillaume mentioned.

André inspected it closely, replying, "Both of our large, heavy-duty suitcases should fit here."

"Surely they will, but it'd help if I see them."

André motioned for Mireille and Ibrahim to exit the car. Both carried the two suitcases stuffed with bills and set them in the trunk of the getaway vehicle.

"Mind if I take a look inside?" Guillaume asked.

"By all means," André answered.

Guillaume unbuckled the latches, flipped the lids open and his eyes scanned the contents that were the wads of bills. He seemed to know what to do, and moved to a tool cabinet, eventually retrieving sets of mechanic uniforms. "Here, let's cover the bills with these. For now, at least." Guillaume lay the sets of immaculately folded uniforms on top of the notes. André counted four pieces of clothing, and Mireille sensed this wouldn't be sufficient to completely obscure the bills. "I have more clothes in my bag," she said.

"We can do away with this if it's not to your liking, prior to crossing the border," Guillaume added.

"We'll see, though it's fine for now," André said.

The two suitcases were placed within the tampered space, well concealed, Guillaume was convinced. Guillaume wasn't finished yet, heading back to the other garage to retrieve two *more* suitcases, making it four in total. He placed these two on the trunk's board, and flipped the lids open. "The entire contents of these two are clothes only, for the purpose of dissuading a border guard from performing a more thorough search of the trunk."

"Smart thinking."

Lastly, Guillaume moved the spare tire to a more appropriate space. Once done, he followed, "Can you provide me the address to the destination?"

André reached for his wallet, retrieving the folded piece

of paper with the written address. He unfolded it and then handed it to Guillaume.

"Fair enough. *West Deutschland.*"

"A land I have never set foot in, hence I rely on you."

"*Avec plaisir. C'est parti.*"

André closed the trunk's lid and everyone got in the car except Youcef, the only one not to join them, who drove off in his own vehicle.

On the road they were, all four in total, heading east in the direction of Alsace, where they planned on making a stop in the city of Strasbourg, prior to crossing the border into West Germany. Ibrahim seemed nervous, anxious by the car traffic in traveling along the highway. In good time, when a road sign indicated that the city of Meaux was in close proximity, he was elated.

"Bless your souls, all of you. I am finally out of the Paris region. You can only imagine how I yearned to be free, to be able to roam about freely on foot again, being confined for several days on end," Ibrahim exclaimed.

"Not to rain on your parade, *monsieur*, but we have several hours of driving ahead of us. Far from roaming about on foot," Guillaume responded.

"I know, but this is a start, and I am ever grateful for this."

André turned to Guillaume. "So what's first, dropping off the money or Ibrahim?"

"Ibrahim first. Under no circumstances are we to come to the border checkpoint with both the dough and him in the vehicle. He'll need to cross the border on his own in a secluded area at night because who knows, perhaps word got out to the border guards at the checkpoint to be on the lookout for someone who fits his profile. Worst-case scenario, it's better that we may potentially face one crime instead of two."

"Crime?" Mireille uttered.

"I use the term 'crime' loosely. Believe me, I wouldn't be getting myself involved in this if I felt that funneling money to the FLN was unmerited or wrongful."

Mireille let out a sigh of relief. "Oh, good. You had me a bit concerned there for a moment."

"At any rate, we'll be fine."

The hours slipped by in traversing the countryside–the regions of Champagne-Ardenne and Lorraine. There was the usual pulling over for fuel and snacks. Mireille and Guillaume spoke of their desire that in ordinary circumstances, they would have ventured off the main highway to stop by a local farm or winery and grab a bottle of wine or cheese from the region, but opted not to, given a fugitive was traveling with them.

The arrival in the outskirts of Strasbourg was at three o'clock in the afternoon. Even being a fair distance away from the heart of the city's medieval urbanscape and famed Gothic cathedrals, André felt kind of struck as though he was no longer in France. Mireille was quick to point out to him a brief history of Alsace and it being former German territory. The choice for a late-afternoon meal was a Strasbourg staple, none other than the classic of the region, *la tarte flambée*, the Alsatian pizza made of *crème fraîche*, caramelized onions and lardons. For André, having ordered his without *lardons*, he was met with a feeling of having committed sacrilege by the server. Nevertheless, the server accommodated him. Ordering to go, Guillaume, Mireille and André joined Ibrahim in the car, opening the pizza box from the backseat. André took one bite, and another. And another. The rich cream, seasoned with nutmeg along with the sweetness of the caramelized onions was like a slice of heaven to him. Tantalizing to his taste buds.

After hanging around the suburbs for a good few hours, nightfall had struck, at a quarter to eight o'clock in the evening. The gang was back on the road, heading north of town. It had only been some forty minutes since leaving the city and Guillaume veered off the main highway, and entered a road, continuing north. He seemed to know exactly where he was going. Now in a more rural setting, he put on the high-beam headlights for improved vision. Vast fields to the left and right, as far as the eye could see, given the darkness. The small town of Scheibenhard was ahead. "We'll be at the Lauter River soon," Guillaume said. "Think of it more like a creek. Your feet will get wet while crossing," he said, speaking to Ibrahim.

"Understood. My double socks and double pants should help," Ibrahim replied.

"When you get off, you'll need to act in haste."

"Like the fugitive I am," Ibrahim remarked, grinning.

The car drove down a quiet residential street of single-family homes, many of which its windows were shuttered. Further down the road, having passed the last of these homes, the fields came into view again and Guillaume immediately turned off the headlights and pulled off the road, onto the grass field. In no time, he brought the car to a stop. The time to make the crossing had arrived.

"Listen: Head straight in the direction I am pointing in and you'll come to a wire fence. The bottom has been cut. Crawl under and through the fence. Then you'll arrive at a small embankment where the river is and where you'll cross on foot. We'll meet you on the other side. Go right now! *Vite!*" Guillaume ordered.

Ibrahim exited the vehicle. A chilly, crisp air permeated. It was cold all right, and he knew what he had to brace for. Ibrahim sprang into action and took off on foot; the car departing seconds later. Not a person could be seen nor heard as he moved about in a rush across the grass-plot. Ibrahim came to the wired fence, diligently combing around, without a flashlight, until finding the cut wire. Utilizing a great deal of arm strength, he bent the wire to the point where he could sneak under. Now down on his knees, Ibrahim successfully crawled his way through, his pants marred by dirt and mud.

Onwards, he didn't have to travel far to come to the embankment where the narrow, relatively shallow river was situated. He searched around for a discarded, large plywood board or the like that could be used as a bridge for crossing–one that was perhaps used by another fugitive who crossed. None was in sight. "Ah, forget it," Ibrahim said to himself. One footstep into the river, and another, his shoes and feet were soaked in icy, soil-streaked stream water, above his ankles. Rather than dwell on it mentally, he rushed in taking the remaining steps needed until crossing the river, making it to the other side. Accomplished! Ibrahim looked up at the night sky and let out a breath of air. He was now standing on West German soil.

Meanwhile, Guillaume pulled to the shoulder of the highway and stopped the car to switch seats with Mireille, in which Mireille would now be the driver. She flipped the vehicle's sun visor to take a look at herself in the mirror, adding some lipstick, as well as donning on her black pea coat. It was evident to André that a big part of Mireille's role in accompanying him on this mission was to sort of seduce or beguile the border guard with her beauty in using her looks as currency to make it easier to cross the border without hassle.

Back on the road, the border checkpoint was only two kilometers away. Guillaume stressed the importance for the three of them to stay calm, and avoid any nervous behavior that would set off a red flag to the border guard. The vehicle pulled up to the border checkpoint, one with a flat roof structure above. Emerging from the patrol booth was a tall, burly guard sporting a navy-blue uniform and a *képi* cap. He approached the driver's door and Mireille fully rolled down the window.

"*Bonsoir*, madame. How's your night going?" the guard asked. He leaned forward, fixing his eyes on her.

"*Bonsoir*, monsieur. All is well. Keeping busy tonight?" Mireille replied.

"It's been a quiet night thus far. May I see your ID?"

"Sure." She reached to her right for her purse, next to the gear shift, retrieving her driver's license and handing it to him.

The guard pointed his flashlight to the ID. "Where are you traveling from?"

"Paris."

"And where exactly are you headed to?"

"Frankfurt," Mireille answered, a bald-faced lie.

The guard took another close look at Mireille's ID, as if he was fixated on her mugshot. "Are you married, madame? Your husband is seated next to you?"

"Oh no, I'm not married. I'm a single woman," she replied with a smile, giving out a suppressed giggle.

The guard handed the ID back to her. Mireille was unable to identify the guard's name on his lapel pin. He pointed the flashlight to the rear driver's side window, and then to André, seated behind Guillaume who was in the passenger's seat. The guard went around the car in André's direction. André rolled his window down and was asked, "May I see your ID?"

"Of course," André replied. He handed it over without hesitation, despite the fact his phony ID listed a domicile in Algeria.

"Algeria, you've come from far. Where have you been staying at?"

"Paris."

"With family? Friends?"

"With my friends here." Even André caught on with telling a lie.

Within seconds, the guard handed the ID back to André. Moving back to Mireille, he asked, "What do you have in the trunk?"

"Oh, our suitcases. Clothes and stuff."

"Can you please pop it open?"

"Yes." Mireille pulled the lever that opened the trunk.

The guard moved towards the trunk. There was a collective holding of the breath by Mireille, Guillaume and André, crossing their fingers that the guard wasn't going to discover the loot and thus commence a lengthy interrogation about it. He flashed the light all around, it seemed. There appeared to be not much to it. Perhaps no more than thirty seconds had passed, and the guard closed the trunk. Facing Mireille once more, he said, "*Avancez*, madame. *Et passez une bonne nuit.*" Have a good night!

"The same to you, monsieur."

Mireille put the car's shift out of the parking gear and cautiously drove at a slow speed while crossing the border, officially entering West Germany. No one had yet to utter a word. Once the border checkpoint was well into the rearview mirror, Guillaume exclaimed, "Whew, success!"

"We did it!" André cried out.

"What a moment!" Mireille admitted.

"Mireille, take the next exit so we can go pick up Ibrahim," Guillaume said. He turned to his left to face her, adding, "He was flirting with you."

"That man had his eyes on you," André followed.

"The fact that he inquired about your marital status, being of no business to him, spoke volumes."

She let out an exhale of pleasure. "Well, I cannot say that this came as a surprise to me."

André unbuckled his seat belt and leaned his head forward, between Mireille and Guillaume, and asked, "Hey, I cannot help but to wonder: Did the guard even search the two suitcases with the loot behind the back seating? I'm not so convinced he did. He might have searched just the other two stuffed with clothes."

"Good point, André. He didn't spend much time at all searching the trunk. It all went by in a flash. Who knows, it could very well be he did not," Guillaume said.

"Which begs the question: Perhaps that guard is a FLN sympathizer? Someone on our side?" Mireille asked.

"Possibly. If he is, and he discovered the loot inside the suitcases, surely he would have understood the purpose and intent behind it, and therefore not question us about it and allow us to easily cross the border without any hassle."

Getting off the next exit, Mireille had to backtrack a bit; Guillaume guiding her every step of the way, en route to the Lauter River. Once again, the car veered off the main road as they now began their search for Ibrahim. Lush green trees abound, Guillaume sensed there could be some trouble in locating him. Mireille flashed the headlights numerous times, in hopes that Ibrahim would notice it. She drove further down a grass field, to the west, and came upon a tractor, flicking on the high-beam headlights. Lo and behold, Ibrahim emerged from behind the tractor, elated to find the gang.

"Success!" Ibrahim exclaimed.

"A smooth crossing, wasn't it?" Guillaume remarked.

"Yeah, pretty much. But my shoes and socks are still wet from crossing the icy water of the river."

"Here," André said, reaching for a pair of shoes and thick socks that were on the floorboard next to his feet.

"Off we go again," Guillaume said. "Let's get the dough deposited into the bank."

André's mission was successfully accomplished. In leaving the funds and subsequent financial affairs in the hands of Omar Touati, a man who was based in Cologne and was a federal committee leader for the French Federation of the FLN, he held the responsibility of initiating the funds transfer to Sofiane. Approximately 2.5 million francs was deposited into a Bank für Gemeinwirtschaft account in Düsseldorf. Thereafter, the funds transfer went to a Société Générale bank account, noting a specified branch located at 11 Boulevard Baudin in Algiers. André, who was paid a sum of 4,500 francs for his overall efforts, accepted the payment without so much as saying a word, as he had no say in the matter. Within days after returning to Paris, André headed back home to Algiers, only bidding farewell to Sami, of all the Parisian contacts he had made.

IV

Whether to his detriment or not, Karim decided to lay low and take a step back from his typical FLN duties and activities, at least temporarily, opting to spend quality time with family. He was glad to be back home in the Casbah of Algiers. During the cool autumn evenings, Karim seldomly ventured outside the neighborhood after nightfall. It was the simple pleasures of being at home at the dinner table with his siblings and mother and sharing a meal; the scent of a couscous topped with sautéed vegetables and fresh, homemade bread that brought much delight to him. Now having the financial means to splurge, he'd also bring home cooked racks of lamb and other fine cuts of meat on occasion for the family.

Karim's absence did not go unnoticed, and one afternoon Sofiane paid him a visit at the Casbah. A brief meeting that mostly consisted of follow-up talk, Sofiane invited

Karim to the hideout at the farmhouse, demanding him to make it for a "meeting amongst associates."

October 20. He was certain that Sofiane was disappointed or angry at him due to his sudden lack of participation in the FLN. In fact, Karim told himself, convinced himself rather, to expect a good scolding from his superior. He left home, picked up a rental car for a couple of days, paid for from the funds he'd received back in West Germany–or, as he called it, the funds from the *suitcase loot*–and took off, heading east of town.

Karim pulled the car in front of the house just after eight o'clock in the evening, the time requested by Sofiane. He knocked on the front door. No answer. After a few tries, Karim reached for the doorknob, and, realizing that it was unlocked, entered the house, finding Sofiane, his back leaning against the kitchen counter.

"Hello Sofiane," Karim said.

Sofiane said nothing, not even acknowledging Karim's presence.

"You've called upon me, and here I am," Karim added.

Sofiane moved towards the sofa, behind it more precisely, and bent down to reach for something. He proceeded to drag a human body, gripping it at the back of the collar, across the living room floor. "Look," he said.

It became evident right away to Karim that it was a dead body. Sofiane released his grip, the body lying face down at the center of the living room floor. He then gave a strong left kick to the head. "Fucking *Harki*," Sofiane said.

"Oh my God," Karim said. He got down to one knee and turned the body face up to learn who it was. "It's

Yassine." Turning to Sofiane, he remarked, "You killed him?"

"Damn right I did."

"Why? What for?" Karim exclaimed, utterly perplexed.

"He's a fucking traitor, so the hell with him." The anger boomed in Sofiane's voice. He picked up a bottle of olive oil and flung it at a wall across the living room, shattering it into shards of glass. Sofiane was in full rage mode.

Karim shook his head. "No, it can't be. How did you learn of this?" he muttered, almost talking to himself, but not low enough of a voice tone as Sofiane still heard him.

"At the office, I stumbled across documents addressing the OAS. As I questioned Yassine, he confessed, after I pretty much intimidated and coerced him for a response I must say, that he had defected to the French side, all the while still working for us, to add insult to injury. *He was finished* right there and then in my book."

"Maybe you have it wrong?–"

"I've nothing wrong! I know exactly what I speak of."

"Did you at least allow him to explain?"

"Karim, he verbally confessed to defecting to the enemy! Nothing more needs to be explained!"

Karim stood silent, allowing him to mentally take in everything.

Sofiane continued, "Can you imagine all the secrets he revealed to the enemy about how we operate, and how damaging that can be for us?"

"No kidding. This is serious."

"I entrusted this man with so much–my personal and business affairs, let alone FLN matters. He was the man I turned to. And this is how he repays me?"

"He became such a good friend to me."

"Well, all of that means nothing now."

"No, I'm sure with all of the money that I helped to get into your hands, you've enriched yourself immensely, and most likely you eliminated someone who you saw as a direct threat to your power and influence."

"Oh bullshit, Karim! Save it! I'd take all that money and set it on fire so long as our destiny becomes fulfilled, and you know that!"

"I can't believe this. After all I've done for you, and this is how you respond?–"

"This isn't about you, Karim! Do you not understand? This is about our movement, and how far we've come in our fight, our struggle. And now he decides to become a turncoat? Treasonous!" Sofiane turned around for a brief moment, only to turn back to facing Karim. "And you better not follow suit and do the same."

Karim struggled to come up with a response at first. "I should take that as a threat?"

Sofiane shrugged. "Interpret it however you wish."

Karim dipped his head, soon coming to a realization. "Well, it looks like my work here is done." He turned around and slowly walked out the front door.

Sofiane, interpreting the remark as Karim walking out and resigning from his duties with the FLN, followed him, in a plea to him. "Karim, wait. You're not quitting on me, are you? You're still needed. I need you–"

"Get the hell away from me! Don't touch me," Karim responded, flailing his shoulder to get Sofiane's hand off him. He then made it inside the car.

"I still need you. We have much work to be done."

"I'm not in the mood."

"Karim, please."

"Goodbye, Sofiane."

Karim slammed the driver's door and drove off into the night.

The encounter with Sofiane left a bad taste in Karim's mouth. He kept his feelings and emotions bottled up, refraining from discussing the incident with family. Yet, Karim felt the desire to speak to the only other person within the FLN whom he had close working relations with, and that was Djamila, the woman who accompanied him in carrying out the *L'Écho d'Alger* bombing, and who served as both a liaison and a nurse. Moreover, she was someone who worked in close connection with all three men–Sofiane, Yassine and Karim.

The following week, Karim arranged a meeting with Djamila, who promised to meet up with him later "after running a few important errands across town." At eight o'clock in the evening, Karim waited for her on the seafront street of Boulevard de la République. She arrived within minutes, wearing a long black skirt and a pale brown blouse under a lightweight coat, finding Karim whose back was leaning against the balustrade railing.

"Here I am, Karim. It seems like we don't see each other much," Djamila said, "but I welcome the occasion when you wish to speak to me."

"I've seen better days," Karim replied, dispirited.

"What do you mean? Is there something wrong?"

Karim let out a sigh, then shook his head. "Shameful. Disgraceful."

"What? Tell me what's going on?"

"It sounds like you're not aware of it, but…Yassine is dead."

"Dead? Really?" she replied, stunned. "Are you serious?"

"He's dead."

"How did you learn of this?"

"I saw his dead body at the farmhouse. Sofiane killed him."

"Oh my God. For what? I just don't understand why."

"For being a *Harki*; a traitor. Apparently, he defected to the enemy side."

Djamila was taken aback, and whispered some words to herself.

"I just walked out and left. I couldn't take being in Sofiane's presence anymore," Karim added. "This doesn't make any sense to me at all, really. Something just doesn't add up. Frankly, I'm just not buying Sofiane's story."

"What do you suspect *did* happen?"

"I suspect both may have clashed due to money and influence. A power struggle, or a power grab."

Djamila, looking away for a moment, then turned her head to face him. "Karim, what will you do now?"

He shrugged, taking a few steps away, and then turning back. "The same thing I have been doing...but I've no intention whatsoever on seeing nor speaking to Sofiane."

"This also brings forth the question as to what I should do as well."

"Talk about an inopportune time for this to happen."

"Wrong time."

"We have an enemy, the OAS, that is more and more emboldened, launching attacks on innocent civilians; and now ourselves, our cause, has taken a huge blow with in-fighting going on." Karim continued, "Sofiane is right about one thing though: We've come too far in our movement, our cause. I just cannot abandon my duties. At this point, it would be too cowardly for me to do so."

"I think you're right; you've done so much for the cause. You're making the right decision."

"Well anyway, let's clear our minds from all of this. I'd love nothing more than to sit down and have a drink and a bite to eat."

"How about we head over to a café nearby?"

"Gladly. Let's go."

Karim and Djamila set off to depart the scene. A gang of three European youths, all males, were walking in the direction towards them; a rowdy, flamboyant bunch. The one closest to Karim was smoking, exhaling a puff of smoke. As soon as the man crossed their path, he shoulder checked Karim, who took offense to it right away; a deliberate act. "What the hell are you up to, punk?" Karim remarked.

"You don't belong here, *bougnoule*," the young man responded.

"Yeah, this is my home, my land. We're reclaiming what is ours."

"That day won't come." The thug took a couple of steps forward, as if looking to start a confrontation.

Djamila sensed the situation was about to escalate and intervened, grabbing Karim by the arm, and pulling him towards her. "Karim, don't. It's not worth it. Let's go."

"You and your kind, your days are numbered," Karim said.

"Far from it."

The other two young men stepped in, and pulled their friend away to prevent anything from getting out of hand. Before walking away, the young thug uttered another racial slur.

"Fucking scumbag," Karim said. He departed the

scene, alongside Djamila. They looked over their shoulder to see that they weren't being followed. Karim led the way, heading in the direction of home. "Let's go to the Lower Casbah." Treading on foot, onto the Rue du Vieux Palais, lay the famous Moorish-style fountain where one would wash their hands via a faucet, and Karim always had a habit of doing so when passing through this street. The two entered Café Malakoff. The tiled walls and high ceilings added to the place's uniqueness and charm. Adjacent to the counter, a live band was on scene, playing *chaabi* music.

Karim and Djamila were seated promptly. Coca-Cola and lemonade were the choice of drinks, to go with *kemia*, North African appetizers served in mezze-style copper bowls. Among them ordered: an assortment of olives, boiled carrot slices later mixed in melted butter, and tomato chunks seasoned with spices.

"Well, we've come this far at least. Let's drink to that," Karim said, clinking his glass with hers.

"And to pray to Allah for protection and blessings moving forward," Djamila replied.

"It's funny though, my own siblings have to remind me to pray, something I've done little of lately, and most certainly didn't do while in Paris." He reached for two pitted green olives and popped them in his mouth.

"Well, you've got to make time for it. Find time for it, I should say. Someway, somehow."

"There's really no excuse for it."

"Oh, speaking of Paris, you haven't told me about your brief stint there." A fork in hand, Djamila stabbed a few slices of the carrots and ate them.

"The right people seemed to fall right into my lap."

"The FLN in France?"

"Yeah, as well as sympathizers who are actually French.

People more experienced than me, and provided me the assistance needed. Hence, I was able to successfully carry out my missions. Without question, it would not have been possible without them. But you know, I never got the vibe that it was a place I could ever feel at home, or even call home, despite the number of Algerians living there, and they are in the tens of thousands, if not hundreds of thousands."

"Of course. Algiers is etched in your heart."

The band concluded a song, met with a rousing applause, and commenced playing another.

"I'm going to tell you this; and I feel I have enough trust in you to share it: I played a role in the transport of a hefty sum of funds–millions of francs–out of France, and ultimately into the hands of Sofiane–"

"Millions of francs, you say?" Djamila interjected, cutting Karim off.

"Yes. I can't help but to wonder if Yassine found out about the millions of francs sent to Sofiane, and perhaps the two got into a spat over finances?" Karim continued.

"Could be. You make a good point. What's your understanding as to what the funds were for?"

"Arms purchases."

"I see."

"Who knows if we'll ever learn the truth of what took place between the two of them." Karim spooned some of the spiced tomatoes and ate them. He continued, "Djamila, listen to me. This is my advice to you: Stick to what you've been doing. Continue with your role acting as a liaison, but more importantly, serving as a nurse. Now if you ever feel that Sofiane is personally threatening you, or harassing or intimidating you, then by all means walk out and quit, for your own safety and well-being. But it goes without saying, your services are very much needed. And you know well better than me as to the situation, the outlook in terms of injuries to ALN soldiers."

"I know, I am very much needed," Djamila replied. "But, in the event I have to walk away and quit, it would be such a huge letdown to those whom I have direct involvement with…and to think that I would then have to justify flat out quitting."

"You don't need to justify anything to anyone, except perhaps me, being that we are associates; collaborators, if you will, hence I am not saying this arrogantly. Follow your heart; follow your gut feeling if you sense that something doesn't seem right."

Djamila gave a nod of the head. It was at this moment that she saw Karim as a dear friend, and perhaps something even more. "I'm glad to have this conversation with you; grateful for it in times like this."

"Do know that if you ever need someone to talk to, I'm here for you."

"Thank you, Karim."

"As for me, I'll continue on as a lone operative, in that I won't be reporting to nor answering to anyone; that is, any superiors. I will be calling the shots as to how I operate. But that being said, both of us have got to work closer together moving forward. This is not the time for us to become distant towards each other; for our working relationship to fade away. Can I hear from you, in your own words, that we'll work closer together from here on out?"

"I am in agreement, Karim."

Hearing that confirmation from Djamila was a pleasing sign of encouragement, a reassurance that Karim had a partner to turn to when needed. In a shift of music style, the musicians on scene now moved onto playing *Bambino* from Lili Boniche, a song that Karim instantly recognized. A pair of couples rose from their seats to dance.

Karim stretched his hand out, towards Djamila. "May I have this dance, *mademoiselle*?"

She blushed; a lovely smile graced her face. "With pleasure."

Karim led her in front of the musicians, closest to the one clutching the *oud*. At first, no physical touching between the two; just moving to the music and voicing the lyrics. As the song progressed, he faced Djamila, and stepping closer to her, took both of her hands, holding her while in motion. She took delight in Karim's boldness, rather than be put off by it. The song soon concluded, with the musicians being met by a warm applause by the patrons.

It was getting late, and upon leaving the café, Karim offered to accompany Djamila in catching a taxi back to her place, to ensure she'd get home safely, to which she agreed. Djamila lived with her parents and didn't seem to have any concern at all regarding the hour she was returning home as she'd often spend days, and even more, out of town when carrying out her nursing duties. When the taxi arrived in front of her apartment at Rue Adolphe Blasselle in Belcourt, Karim turned to Djamila and said, "Remember what I said. I strongly urge you to follow my advice."

"Don't worry, Karim. You have my word," she replied.

The several weeks that passed gave way to the year 1962. A reality that became more and more apparent was a government, and the law enforcement authorities, whose actions were inadequate in combating the OAS savagery, in spite of its measures taken. Even the numerous checkpoints throughout the city did little to deter the OAS. The overall comportment of the Algérois around town struck Karim as a tad out of the ordinary; a people surely apprehensive of what lurked around every street corner, or behind them. Or, in addition, simply weary and fed up with the lengthy war and ineffective governance, not to mention lawlessness in general. The two adversaries to the Algerian fight for independence, the OAS and the French government, were bound to clash with each other this year, Karim was convinced.

January 3. Karim left home, en route to the Sidi Ramdan Mosque. Along the passage, a stray cat or two here and there, searching for any scraps of food they could find. Looking above, a common sight for the Casbah resident– articles of clothing hanging on clotheslines, attached with clothespins, and open window shutters. Just outside the mosque, one could catch a sublime view overlooking not only the city, but the Bay of Algiers as well. Karim always took a moment to stop and admire the beauty of it all. As was customary procedure, Karim removed his shoes prior to setting foot inside the mosque. In a matter of seconds, Malika, one of his neighbors, was on her way out the door.

"Ah, Malika. What a time for us to cross paths," Karim said.

"I just finished my prayer, Karim. And you're about to start yours?" she replied.

A nod of the head by Karim. "These days, me attending a mosque, it's for being in great need."

"Oh, my. What for?"

"Guidance, wisdom, direction."

"I see, that's more than fair. And nothing out of the ordinary. I'd have thought you've been backsliding."

"I have been." He looked over to his right, and turned back to face Malika. "Let's move over to the corner there." She followed him, both treading softly on the maroon carpet, to a corner, allowing for more privacy between the two. Only three other people were seen inside the mosque, all prostrating, engaged in the act of prayer. Malika, rather plump and tall as well, wore a full white burka. Karim, focusing on the enameled-silver bracelet with elaborate designs that looked to be of Imazighen origin on her left wrist, asked, "I take it one of the neighbors made that for you?" Small talk.

"Certainly. And I return the favor. It's kind of like we barter with each other." Ensuring no one else was within earshot, Malika continued, "Speaking of neighbors, it has been made known to me that some of them are upset with the whole current state of affairs in the city, and are eager to take action."

"Really?" Karim answered, surprised. "On the side of the FLN?"

"Of course, Karim. What other side?"

"It's not so obvious to me, Malika." Karim now brought his tone of voice to just above a whisper, adding, "Do you realize how many traitors there are? *Harkis*, as they're called? Those who have been captured, they're even being executed by the ALN itself, at the behest of the commanders."

"No, it sounds rather foreign to me. But what I speak of, it's those in alliance with our fight, our battle for independence. And I'm sure this can be verified."

"Understood then," Karim answered, sounding a bit relieved. "But it sounds as though they don't know who or what to turn to?"

"That's how it seems like to me."

"Have you any names to give?"

"Start with Anissa," Malika replied, "she's the number one person to go to."

"Wonderful. Listen, I'm going to set about my purpose for being here and get into prayer."

"No worries, I won't hold you back."

"Much appreciated, Malika. May you be blessed."

There was no sign of the neighbor Anissa later that day nor the next. A knock on her door yielded nothing. Karim assumed that either he simply happened to pass by at the wrong time, or she might have been out of town. The following day, Karim rented a car yet again. He sensed he'd be utilizing a vehicle more often henceforth. It was always the same deal at the car rental agency; the European employees in astonishment at how a young Algerian possessed the financial means to rent a vehicle, and on several occasions for that matter. Needing to park the car closer to home for obvious reasons of safety, he found a convenient parking spot just off Rue Randon, well past La Grande Synagogue d'Alger, but within distance of the Marché de la Lyre. Karim felt more at ease in leaving the vehicle parked in the Jewish district of town. For one, the Jews had never harassed him in any form. Secondly, he preferred to avoid leaving the car on one of the main streets near the seafront where he could potentially encounter trouble from a European discovering *a young bougnoule driving a nice Volkswagen.*

January 9. Karim sought to pay Zineb a visit at the clandestine FLN office in El-Biar, but opting to take a different route by first passing through Bab-el-Oued. Moving past the neighborhood led to an uphill, rugged road towards the quarries that were known as the Carrières Jaubert. To Karim's right, he could see the massive quarry, with diggers and other laborers hard at work, extracting minerals and other valuable resources. Just off the side of the road, a throng of Algerian men, sporting white burnouses, swarmed the vehicle, causing Karim to slam on his brakes. A few of the men tapped on the windows. Although startled to a degree, Karim rolled down the driver's side window just a crack to be able to hear them speaking.

"Sir, we're strong, able-bodied, and willing. We need work. Hire us, please," one of the men said.

"Sorry, guys. I'm not an employer."

"Anything, sir. We'll take it, we need the money," he pleaded.

Karim expressed his inability to help them once more. He immediately thought of the similar encounter he had with Mehdi and his pals. Feeling sympathy, he wished he could help them in any way, if only he had the means to. "Will you men congregate here tomorrow?"

"Yes. We're here every day, seven days per week."

"I really wish I could help in some way. But now I know that if I am able to, I know where to find you men."

"Yes, of course. You'll find us here."

Karim rolled up the window, only to have the same man give a few knocks on the window, this time making Karim a bit irritated.

"Listen, there's a checkpoint ahead. If you want to avoid it, you should turn around now and head back in the direction you came from," the man said.

"Damn it," Karim muttered. "Will do, I'll avoid it." He made a U-turn, as soon as the men cleared the way, avoiding potential hassle and trouble.

In a change of plans, Karim dismissed paying Zineb a visit and opted to go straight to see Sebastián at his law office. A short drive from the Chemin des Carrières and down the Boulevard de Champagne took him near the Avenue des Consulats. After parking the car two blocks away from the address, he went on foot to the law office. About halfway there, Karim spotted a handwritten notice on a building wall, next to a pharmacy. The notice was secured by duct tape and written with a black marker, its author direct with his or her message:

> *To all Europeans of French Algeria,*
>
> *May you heed this call to join in the fight for our rights. De Gaulle and his government are betraying us. Down with de Gaulle! You, of European stock, your battle is our battle! The OAS stands with you and fights for you. We the Europeans built modern-day Algeria and we will not give it up without a fight. The FLN will be crushed!*
>
> *To victory, our fellow citizens!*
>
> *OAS*

The immediate, instinctive reaction from Karim was to yank that notice and tear it into pieces, but he knew better. Should a European passerby witness such an act, it could possibly lead to a brutal beating, or even worse, and hence it was best to avoid such a scenario. Even looking around, Karim wasn't the only one present; a handful of pedestrians were walking about.

He arrived at the address and ascended the stairwell to the second floor. Karim was greeted by the receptionist, Mademoiselle Lavoie, who informed him that "Sebastián has stepped out of the office. He should be back shortly. Would you like to wait until he returns?"

To which Karim answered, "yes." Seated in a comfy bergère chair adjacent to the door, several minutes passed, with Karim glancing at Mathilde every now and then. No sign of Sebastián. Continuing to wait, Karim soon looked at the clock on the wall behind the receptionist's desk and close to an hour had passed. Finally, Sebastián arrived, and he quickly summoned Karim into his office.

"Where have you been?" Karim asked him.

"Oh, I was at the Cinéma Majestic," Sebastián answered.

Karim was sort of dumbfounded. "On a Tuesday afternoon?"

"Why yes, my client canceled his appointment, so since I had time to kill, I figured I'd go catch a flick. I understand you've been waiting for me."

"For a good hour, I'd say."

"Well you know, they don't tell you at the start of a film what the duration of it will be. It turned out to be longer than I expected."

"Listen, I was just at the Carrières Jaubert and came upon a throng of unemployed Algerian men seeking work. Have you any idea where I can send them for work? Anyone you know who'd hire them?"

"Ah, the Carrières Jaubert. A place I will always have a connection to. I told you about my father's story. What were you doing there?"

"Taking a joyride, I guess."

"Very well. Yes, you can take them to the Saint-Eugène Stadium. I hear there's some kind of renovating going on and they're looking for laborers."

"Excellent. That's just what I needed, and I'm sure they

will be pleased with it. This is something kind of sentimental to me. I found myself in the same situation this past summer and was unable to help out a group of unemployed men who were seeking work. I'm motivated to deliver this time and assist my fellow Algerians."

"You're not going there right after you leave here, are you?"

"No, it's too late in the afternoon. I'll try back again tomorrow." Karim now sat in a more upright position, continuing, "By the way, this is just between you and me: During my stay in Paris, I was given a decent sum of money for my efforts, hence why I'm able to afford to rent a car, for whatever length of time as needed. I could be in this all for myself, enrich myself, but I'd rather help out my people. You understand, don't you?"

Sebastián dipped his head while nodding a few times, in full agreement. "You're fighting the good fight, Karim. And you should be proud of what you're doing. Nothing more needs to be said."

"So how's business been lately?"

"Kind of slow, given the time of year. But I'm charging my clients a higher rate for my services. On another note, just yesterday, a friend of mine, a wealthy Maltese businessman, informed me that he's closing his business and leaving Bab-el-Oued, and fleeing Algeria for that matter, to move back to Malta."

In hearing this, it was if an alarm was set off to Karim. "The writing is on the wall?"

Sebastián puffed. "I'm expecting we're going to see more of this in the near future."

A knock on the door was followed by Mathilde entering the office. She handed Sebastián a note written on a page torn out of a desk calendar before walking out of the office.

"Oh my, I forgot. Karim, I'd like to kindly request a huge favor of you: Can you swing by the post office right away, before it closes for the day, and get a cashier's check or money order? It's for a referral fee that I must pay," Sebastián said.

"Sure thing, consider it done," Karim replied.

"I have to send the payment out as soon as possible. Since my bookkeeper does not return until Thursday from his Corsican vacation, the transaction will have to be done 'off the books.' For now at least." Sebastián pulled out a wad of bills from his front left pocket, secured with a money clip. He removed the clip and peeled off several bills, then counting them. "Here's 175 francs exact." He then peeled off one more bill. "Here's a 10-franc note. Treat yourself to a nice dinner tonight."

"How kind of you," Karim said, reaching for the bills. Within moments, he headed out the door to take care of the errand.

After taking care of business for Sebastián, Karim returned to the Casbah in the evening hour. On the very street of his residence, Rue N'Fissa, a little boy around seven years of age, Ferhat, was dribbling a soccer ball, playing by himself. The boy was the son of Anissa, so Karim was assured he would come across her at any moment. Karim joined in, kicking the soccer ball back and forth with the youngster, entertained, like a kid lighting up inside a confectionery. Given Karim's age, he could have very well passed as an older brother to the boy.

Some ten minutes later, Anissa appeared. In her late twenties, she wore a red, buttoned kaftan with floral patterns, and was breastfeeding a baby, secured by a nursing cloth. Karim approached her and said, "Lately I haven't seen you around."

"Why yes, here's the reason why," Anissa replied, gesturing to her baby, letting out a giggle.

"Congratulations. I'm sure he or she will bring an abundance of joy to your life."

"Thank you. It's a girl. Her name is Yazmin."

"I heard from Malika of word that some neighbors are interested in getting involved in battle, and joining the FLN? Is that right?"

"Well, here it is; what I've been told: There's a man who is a bombmaker. He's seeking to strike enemy targets."

"Any knowledge or specifics on the bombs themselves?"

"From what I hear, grenades and other handheld explosives. But there may very well be more that he makes. There are other people at his side, eager to join in."

"Where is this man?"

"I'd have to show you his hideout. He operates out of a safe house. It's pretty discreet, and anyone, any passerby, can easily overlook it."

"Sounds intriguing. Mind if you take me there?"

"Sure, of course. But can I take you there at a later time?" Anissa caressed her newborn daughter. "As you can see, I'm breastfeeding."

"That's fine with me."

"Oftentimes, he's not available in the daytime. Your best bet to get ahold of him is in the evening or late at night."

"Fair enough. When you're ready, take me there. You know where to find me."

The next day around the mid-morning hour, Karim left

home and drove back to the quarry in the outskirts of town, determined to follow through and provide the unemployed men with much-desired work. A pleasant, warm, sunny day in January, Karim arrived at the same spot, more or less, as he did the last time, and sure enough the throng of men descended on his car once Karim came to a full stop. At that moment, something caught him as odd, unique. One of the men was sporting a pale turtle green cap that looked to possibly be an ALN army cap. Otherwise, he was wearing just casual slacks and a shirt, but the cap stood out above all. Karim was eager to learn more about this man.

Karim got out of the car, the men with their hands raised, hoping to be selected. "I can only fit four of you in my car. I'll take you three men, the three closest to the rear right door," he said. The men wasted no time in opening the rear door and hopping in. "And you, wearing the cap. I want you!" he added, pointing at him.

"Me?" the man responded, stunned.

"Yes, you. Take the passenger's seat."

The stranger got in the seat, and Karim drove off. He sought to have a private, one-on-one talk with this stranger, but it wasn't the ideal time nor place, given the other passengers in the car. Hence, Karim had to wait until arriving at the stadium. The car ride was rather calm and tranquil. Karim mentioned "Saint-Eugène" to them, but didn't say a word about the stadium. He drove past the Maillot Military Hospital and onto the seafront street that was Boulevard Pitolet. A rolldown of the window by the man seated in the passenger's seat brought forth a cool, crisp sea breeze that circulated inside the car.

Karim pulled over and came to a stop, close to the stadium's entrance. Two European men, dressed professionally, were engaging in dialogue with each other–with one man clutching onto a large, tall sheet of paper that was rolled up, perhaps an architect's rendering or sketch of some kind. Both men looked to be the right ones to contact. "Go speak to those two men. They should point you in the right direction," Karim told the men in the back. They did so, getting out of the vehicle, as did the other man seated in the passenger's seat, but Karim made it a point to quickly get ahold of him. Getting out of the car, Karim got his attention. "Listen, I'd like to have a talk with you."

"But I need to join the other men," he uttered.

"This is something important. It won't take much of your time, and I'll bring you back. If not, I'll compensate you for a day's wages. You have my word. Deal?"

"All right then." The man got back in the car, as did Karim, and he drove off.

"Where are we going?" the stranger asked, in his forties or so, with short black hair, though wavy on the top, and a bushy mustache.

"We're just taking a stroll," Karim answered. "I have to ask you: Your cap looks like that worn in the ALN. Are you a current or former ALN soldier?"

"Former," the man acknowledged.

"Former soldier?" Karim uttered.

"Yes. And you are? A good Samaritan? An undercover *flic*? I can't tell where your allegiance lies."

"Consider me a good Samaritan. I wear that with a badge of honor, albeit with a sense of humility at the same time. But moreover, I am a FLN operative."

"Pleased to hear it. You had me worried there for a moment."

"Don't worry, I'm not some stealth agent who's secretly working for the colonialist cause, if that's what you were wondering."

"Clarification is always a good thing. I'm glad you cleared the air on that. You sure do have this interrogatory nature about you. That's not to say it's a good or bad thing though, it's just what my senses are picking up."

"Understood. I would like to know, were you discharged or did you quit?"

"I quit."

"What for, may I ask?"

"The commander insulted my tribe."

"Oh my, that's terrible." Karim replied, taken aback by the comment. "Just awful. And your tribe is?"

"Chaoui. Don't ask me to repeat the insult, because I won't."

"Sorry to hear that," Karim added, shaking his head.

"It angered me a great deal, obviously, and still does when I think of it. And to make matters worse, it was mentioned to me by two comrades that the commander acquired a seafront villa—no word as to where. So he finds it worthy to basically enrich himself and set himself up to live a life of luxury at some point, while disparaging our ethnic backgrounds, not to mention at times, having an indifferent attitude towards us soldiers, those of us who're doing the real work on the ground? That's not right, and totally unacceptable to me."

"Oh no," Karim mumbled. *This sounds eerily familiar*, he thought. *Where have I seen this before?* He could not help but to think of Sofiane, serving his own self-interests, acting in self-aggrandizement. "And so you left the rural area to come out here?"

"I needed to get away, and moreover, to find work close to or in a metropolitan city. It's been a struggle though, in that regard, as I'm sure you can tell. Hence, here I am."

"Where are you staying at?"

"In Telemly. A kind soul opened up their home to me. It's not the ideal place. It's really a basement and the conditions are unpleasant–peeled, chipped plaster, among other things–but it'll do for now at least." The man finally introduced himself as Noureddine.

Karim headed straight to Algiers to spend some time to get to better know Noureddine as he was not going to drop him off back at the stadium. After parking the car, the two strolled along the bustling Rue Randon, passing by produce stalls and aggressive merchants selling brass and silver kitchenware, as well as other household goods. On a nearby street, they entered a small, family-run restaurant to have lunch–*dobara*, a chickpea stew in a rich tomato sauce, drizzled with a generous amount of olive oil and topped with chopped parsley, alongside *mhadjeb*, flatbread stuffed with vegetables. Glasses of water sufficed for drinks. Noureddine, it turned out, was a bricklayer by trade, and who, in joining the ALN, gained firsthand experience in handling weaponry, including grenades and bombs, which, ironically, were the weapons of choice by the OAS for inflicting damage on their adversaries.

"How did you come about getting a car?" Noureddine asked.

"Oh, I'm renting it. I certainly didn't purchase it," Karim answered.

"Well even then, it's still something. You can get around town and elsewhere with more ease."

Karim then shrugged his shoulders. "I'm fortunate money has made its way to me. And even by chance, I guess you can say." A vague response. He tore the *mhadjeb* in half and then folded one piece, taking a big bite. "But otherwise, I had a falling-out with my former boss, and our working relationship has been severed. I'm now more than convinced that he's in it all for himself, similar to what you were telling me earlier."

"Most of them are. Heck, I wouldn't be surprised if it's all of them; that includes the FLN leaders as well. Do you know that many members of the Provisional Government, each of them have a net worth of millions of francs?"

Karim's jaw almost dropped at what he'd heard. "Millions you say?"

"Yes. They're all living the good life behind the scenes."

"Who told you all this?"

"The same former comrades I was telling you about earlier. Now how they learned of all this is beyond me."

"And you didn't press them about it to get more details?"

"No. And in hindsight, I should have. I regret doing so." Noureddine took in another spoonful of the chickpeas. "Not to get ahead of ourselves here, but I suppose once the war is over, these members of the present Provisional Government, they will truly live like kings."

Karim sat still, reflective, although not envious nor bitter in any way. "Sofiane showed his true hand."

"I bet he didn't even compensate you."

"No, he *did* compensate me. On a monthly basis."

"How much did he pay you?" Noureddine asked, inquisitive.

"Not much," Karim replied, choosing not to state a dollar amount. "But for a once-penniless teenager, it was an enormous financial blessing to me. However, that financial blessing is now a thing of the past. Ever since our falling-out, Sofiane stopped paying me remuneration, and rightfully so as I no longer work for him." He then took the other piece of *mhadjeb* and dunked it in the rich tomato sauce of the stew, finishing it with a few bites.

"Don't let any of this dishearten nor demoralize you in any way."

"Do I feel like a fool for my involvement, my participation over the course of many months? No, not really, to be frank. We still have a goal to attain, and we must keep our eyes on the prize; and that is to be free from colonial rule and live in an independent Algeria."

"Bless you, Karim. Your mindset is in the right place."

Karim downed the remaining water in his glass. In being reminded of Noureddine's experience with weaponry, Karim invited him to meet up later. "Come join me tonight at the Casbah. If everything goes as planned, both of us will be collaborating; for the foreseeable future, I hope."

It was past seven o'clock. Nightfall had set in on the city. Karim picked up Noureddine in front of his residence and then headed right back in the direction he came from. After parking the car in the now-usual spot off Rue Randon, the two went on foot to the Casbah. As advised by Anissa, Karim sought to visit the bombmaker whom she spoke of, at this time of day, at night, in hopes of finally being able to see him. *Voilà*, he recalled the right passage, close to the cemetery, where cobblestone stair steps led down to a barred door. A light was seen through a concealed window, suggesting that someone was present inside. Karim gave a firm knock on the wooden door, and then another. A man came to the door, opening it just slightly to see who it was. "Can I help you?" he asked.

"Anissa sent me. I'd like to have a word with you," Karim replied.

"Your name?"

"Karim."

The man looked over at Noureddine, curious. "And you are?" he followed.

Before Noureddine could even answer, Karim jumped in and responded, "My associate."

He looked back at Karim, now convinced, it seemed. "Come on in," the man said, opening the door all the way. The moment Karim and Noureddine entered, he closed the door securely shut. "Follow me," he added, leading the men down a narrow corridor and to a room. "This is my lair, as I like to call it."

The place was candlelit, small, with a sturdy wooden desk–untidy and unorganized–as evidenced by the contents on top of it, which clearly featured bombmaking parts and paraphernalia. An Algerian flag hung on the wall to the right. "I've no additional chairs here," the man said.

"No worries, we don't mind standing," Karim replied. He looked over at the desk and saw a wooden box, that more or less resembled a wooden shoe box, and inside it appeared to also be parts of a bomb. Another smaller box was just beside it, but he couldn't get a closer look at it.

"The bombs that I assemble here, it is my aim to make good use of these. That is to say, to assign the handling of these bombs to men who can be relied upon, who know what they're doing, and to strike enemy targets. Heck, I don't even mind doing it myself, but I'd like to get advice from some strategic minds first; those who've combed the city, are familiar with its 'hot spots,' and have studied and identified enemy targets to strike."

"Well, you're looking at the right men to get the job done."

"That's what I like to hear." The man finally gave his name–Hocine. In his late fifties or so, he wore reading glasses, had gray hair with sparse balding at the top of his head, as well as a full, thick goatee. He gave off the air of a man who was meticulous in the approach of his craft; one who didn't rush through things and labored with diligence until fully satisfied with the end result.

Karim shifted his eyes to the Algerian flag hanging on the wall. "I don't even need to bother asking where your allegiance lies."

"No need to. But for good measure, I'll summarize it in one sentence: I cheered and wholeheartedly supported the All Saints' Day attack, and my position hasn't changed since."

"Wow, seven-plus years."

"Seems a hell of a lot longer than that if you ask me." Hocine looked up at Karim, and then Noureddine. "And what are your credentials, your backgrounds, the two of you?"

Karim raised his left hand, stating, "FLN operative," with Noureddine following suit, answering, "former ALN soldier."

"Very well then. Two men experienced in taking action against the enemy." Hocine faced his desk. "I still need to fiddle with this explosive here. I'll come back to it later." He pushed the box aside and focused on the other, which was the assemblage of a hand grenade. Hocine took hold of it, and a spare part that was *la goupille*, the pin.

"Careful now, I don't want myself to be found in bits and pieces," Karim said, a rather amusing remark.

Hocine grinned, not saying anything at first, only to later remark, "It's in good hands." A kind of *been there, done that* expression in handling explosives. He bent down to reach the desk's drawer at the bottom, pulling out a uniform–neatly folded and ironed–, followed by a mail satchel. Hocine then rose and handed them to Karim.

"Here, the clothes are a mailman's uniform. Don't ask me how I obtained it. Use it as a disguise when entering an establishment of your desired target."

Karim took the outfit and gently put it inside the satchel, which he then strapped over his shoulder.

Hocine continued, "Several explosives over here are fully assembled and ready for use. You can take them now, or come back later for them."

"We can–"

Noureddine cut Karim off. "Allow me to take the lead on this," he said.

Nothing more needed to be said. Noureddine wanted to take on the task, and Karim left it in the hands of a more experienced bomb handler. The two left the safe house and into the night, the streets emptied of children, all whom were within the confines of home.

"You'll need to advise me where it is best to strike," Noureddine said.

"Which I'll be glad to. It's best for a newcomer in town to not try to figure it out on his own, and you have me for that," Karim replied.

February 5. It was long overdue for Karim to pay Zineb a visit at the clandestine FLN office. In the early afternoon hour, Karim got in the Volkswagen and drove off. Arriving at the front door of the office, Karim knocked and was met warmly by Zineb.

"Oh Karim, am I glad to see you," she said, giving him a hug as well.

"Really? For what cause?" he replied.

"It gets lonely around here, and I just miss your presence and conversing with you."

"Oh, well that explains it. But yes, without Yassine around, I can imagine so."

"I've someone else to work with here; a replacement, that is to say. He's not here at this moment. It's not the same though, I must admit, but I've gotten used to it."

"Has Sofiane stopped by here recently?" Karim asked, taking a seat on a swivel chair.

"Yes. Once last month, and again about two weeks ago."

"And?"

"He was calm, tact, and gave me a cashier's check for my service. But he combed through Yassine's desk, the drawers, file cabinets and the shelf, as if he was looking for something specific."

"Hmm, that's one of the reasons why I came by. Did he mention what he was looking for?"

"No. I just sat helplessly by until he was finished."

"I also felt the need to stop by because I had doubts that you might still be working here; that you might've quit."

"Oh no, this is a job I made a commitment to, and I've got to carry out my duties, whether short-staffed or not."

"It takes a strong woman to retain that commitment, Zineb, and I'm proud of you for sticking through amidst the rifts and in-fighting."

"That means a lot to me, Karim."

"It's the same thing I told Djamila; for her not to walk out and quit. And by all appearances, she has heeded my advice."

Karim moved to one of the filing cabinets and opened a drawer.

"What are you looking for?" Zineb asked.

"Any clues that can be found regarding Yassine."

"By all means."

Karim pulled out a manila folder. In it was several documents.

"Oh, I should point out: A week before I last saw him, he mentioned of an upcoming interview with a Le Figaro correspondent. Don't know what to make of it. Take it for what it is."

Karim was taken aback. "Le Figaro correspondent?... Hmm, I wonder why."

Zineb shrugged her shoulders. "He didn't say."

Karim fingered another folder in the file cabinet, and skimmed through page after page of what looked to be drafts of communiqués. Nothing out of the ordinary, it seemed.

Zineb took a seat at her desk and began typing on the typewriter.

"What has your focus been on now?" Karim asked.

"Typing newsletters to be distributed to our fellow Algerians out in the *bled*."

Karim moved to the gray steel shelf. A pile of newspapers sat, and he browsed through them, all French newspapers: *Le Figaro, France-Soir, Le Canard Enchaîné.* "These aren't yours, are they?" he asked her. "Or were they Yassine's?"

"Those papers? Those were all his."

"All from the colonialist's point of view; not one from ours." A closer look revealed the date of each paper. "And these are months' old. What are they still doing here?"

"They should've been tossed in the trash bin where they belong, but I just didn't bother, and well, they've all sat there untouched."

Karim decided to stop there with his search efforts, realizing it was a fruitless task. Before leaving the office, he moved towards Zineb and said, "Don't tell Sofiane I was here, OK?"

"Understood."

"As if it wasn't evident already, we had a falling-out."

"I'm sorry to hear that. How are you getting by these days?"

"I've been working alone, and I won't stop what I've been doing."

"Will I see you around?"

Karim nodded his head. "Of course you will."

Noureddine was pleased to share the news with Karim that he succeeded in tossing a grenade into the Brasserie des Facultés, and the detonation as a result. The bombing was a tit-for-tat response to a number of Algerian cafés bombed recently. Noureddine had momentarily scoped out the brasserie first, disguised in a mailman's uniform, clean shaven, and delivered a sole letter—a standard envelope with a FLN tract inside. A fictitious sender's address was used on the top-left corner of the envelope, with the addressee correctly listed as the Brasserie des Facultés to give the notion that he had a legitimate piece of mail to deliver. "I counted sixteen people inside the brasserie," Noureddine acknowledged, prior to walking out the door and tossing the grenade, leaving the place in shambles. Karim responded in commending Noureddine, noting, "I've found the right, trustful partner to collaborate with, in engaging in *fellagha* warfare *dans nos rues d'Alger*. I couldn't be more pleased with you. *And we haven't seen the end yet.*"

March 18. In the early evening, following a routine grocery run, Karim made a quick stop at a *magasin*, whose shopkeeper informed him that the President of the GPRA,

Benyoucef Benkhedda, would be making an announcement "shortly." Given that he had a transistor radio at home, Karim was set to make a dash home. "If I'm unable to tune in due to technical difficulties or whatever, I'll come right back here," he said to the shopkeeper.

He hurried back home, while carrying a shopping bag with two loaves of bread, tomatoes and zucchinis inside. Entering the apartment, Karim went straight to tuning into the transistor radio, the only electronic device he had at home. While preparing a meal alongside his mother and siblings, the time came when the voice of Benkhedda could be heard. Everyone rushed to the transistor radio resting on top of the dining table. Benkhedda officially announced that the Évian Accords had been signed, noting it as a "victory," paving the way for Algerian independence.

Karim gave his mother an elated, jubilant embrace. "Independence is on the horizon," he said.

His mother, Sara, expressed joy. "We've waited long enough. Our time has come!"

"Let me go spread the word to the neighbors."

Karim darted out the door and headed to Anissa's apartment down the street. A couple of neighbors were present. Karim shouted at them, and for all nearby to hear; a cry of victory. He knocked on Anissa's door, and she responded promptly.

"Have you heard? The Évian Accords have been signed! It's a done deal!" Karim said.

"Ah, it's done!" she uttered, giving him a warm hug. "At long last."

The two headed down Rue N'Fissa with Anissa carrying her two-month-old daughter, and her son right beside her. A joyous celebration ensued with other neighbors; cheering, clapping and evoking chants of liberty.

"Awesome, Karim! I bet you're overwhelmed with joy, but relief as well. You've certainly done your share in this fight," Anissa said.

"But there's a sense of unfinished business along with it; I'm not entirely relieved yet," Karim replied.

"Where do we go from here?"

"My opinion? Be vigilant, stay at or around home if at all possible, and take precaution. This announcement is only going to infuriate the enemy, the diehards to be precise, and they'll for sure be seeking retaliation, and, dare I say it, they'll be out for blood."

"Yes, you're right, Karim. Who knows what they're capable of doing."

"This is far from over. We haven't reached the end yet."

"Well noted. I'll stick around here with my kids, for now at least."

"As you should. Let's acknowledge this for what it is: A diplomatic and political victory? Yes. A final victory? No."

A ceasefire commenced at noon the next day, bringing about an end to the hostilities between the French army and the FLN. However, bloodshed did not come to a halt. In fact, violence only escalated, to a new level, at the hands of the OAS, who, struck by betrayal, ignored the ceasefire and sought to sabotage the Évian Accords by any means necessary. The OAS launched terrorist attacks against the police, European civilians looking to leave Algeria–especially by bombing their apartments–and of course Algerians themselves. Just as Karim had expected, a violent clash broke out between the OAS and the French army, in Bab-el-Oued. Karim took note of Sofiane's playbook from back during the putsch the year before, and avoided venturing outside the Casbah for a few days, in case the violence somehow happened to spread to the periphery of the Casbah. Also, it was not his fight, he told himself, understanding that it was apt to let the OAS and the French army settle their scores.

Karim woke up in the morning, lying there in his bed and staring straight at the ceiling, only to sit up and lean his back against the wall moments later. Being cooped up long enough, it was time to step out of the confines of home. His first order of business was to pay a visit to Djamila, whom he last saw prior to the ceasefire. Karim took off in the car and soon arrived at her apartment on Rue Adolphe Blasselle. Knocking on her door, she responded timely.

"Come on in, Karim," Djamila said, opening the door wide open, Karim stepping inside.

"Your place is spotless," he said.

"Oh, it's always like this."

A suitcase rested on top of the sofa, arousing curiosity from Karim.

"Leaving town?" he inquired.

"Possibly. Haven't made a decision yet. Perhaps you can help me solidify my decision."

"Well sure," Karim said.

"I was at the office yesterday with Zineb and a surprise visitor stopped by."

"Surprise visitor? Who would that be?"

"One of the editors of *El Moudjahid*, who came from Tunisia. A man by the name of Chakib Hamzaoui."

"Is that so? So he crossed the border then."

"A charming man, upbeat in light of the recent news; a brilliant mind."

"Did he bring any copies with him?"

"Yes. They're inside the suitcase, and in Arabic print."

Karim moved to the suitcase and unbuckled the latches, flipping the lid open. He took hold of one copy, studying the front page. An ALN soldier carrying a little girl, accompanied by the headline: "*Peuple Algérien.*" Algerian people, followed further down the page with the acknowledgement of the ceasefire and it being: "*Étape vers l'indépendance.*" A step towards independence.

"Several copies as you can see, though the suitcase is not stuffed," Djamila said.

"Did the man distribute any copies on his way to Algiers?"

"Yes, he claims he made stops in Constantine and Kabylia distributing many copies," she replied. "I was thinking of doing the same and distributing them in the *bled*, to those who are not in the know and lack access to the media in hopes that this will encourage, incentivize them to spring into action and to do so in gravitating towards the cities. But these issues are dated the 19th. Given that today's the 24th, the issues are already several days old. What do you think? Should I still distribute them?"

Karim shrugged. "Why not? Better late than never, I suppose. I've a car. I'd be more than willing to do the driving."

"Oh, would you? It'd be much appreciated."

"*Volontiers,*" Karim replied. "In what area did you have in mind?"

"To the west, in the direction of Orléansville, and then perhaps south towards the Atlas Mountains."

In thinking of the first instance where he stumbled upon a copy of *El Moudjahid* newspaper–Les Tailleurs du Monde–, it gave Karim an idea. "But first, I'd like to make a stop elsewhere. The tailor shop where we utilize its storage space to hide weapons. It has been quite some time since I was last there. You're not in an immediate rush to distribute the papers, are you?"

"No, not at all."

Leaving the apartment unit on the second floor, the two descended the staircase and out onto the street. Djamila put the suitcase in the trunk, and off they went. Turning onto the Rue Michelet, Karim proceeded. Having passed Algiers University, a roadblock lay ahead. He could see a fairly large gathering of people in the distance. Pedestrians were moving along the sidewalk and onto the middle of the street itself once past the roadblock. *It's going to be one of those days*, Karim thought. He expected nothing short of a mass demonstration by the pro-*Algérie française* supporters. Moreover, Karim caught a glimpse to his right of the Brasserie des Facultés in its damaged state, bombed weeks earlier by Noureddine.

A peace officer signaled to Karim to turn left, and leave. Karim made a left turn, onto Rue Ballay, and found a parking spot in front of a photo and printing shop, with the Avenue Pasteur ahead of them. Once settled into the spot, Karim brought the car to a complete stop, put the shift into the parking gear and turned off the ignition. "Let's check out what's going on," he said.

"Are you sure we should do this?" Djamila replied, facing him.

"If it's nothing worthwhile, or things get out of hand, we'll leave."

The two exited the car and proceeded on foot to Rue Charles Péguy. Once there, a noticeable police presence was on hand to maintain order. Most of those of Algerian appearance were more on the sidewalk as opposed to the middle of the street, while the Europeans were chanting, voicing their displeasure, as well as their demands.

"Djamila, stick close to me," Karim said. The two moved down the street, no more than a block. At that moment, Karim looked over his shoulder, and a wild melee broke out in the street. By all appearances, it primarily involved the Europeans and the police, although a handful of Algerians were seen in the mix. Karim was alarmed, as was Djamila, and he took her by the hand, contemplating what action to take. To his right, he saw a sign on a building that read "À LOUER." For rent. The sight of such a sign indicated to him that the units on the ground floor as well as those on the floors above were likely vacant. In a bold move, Karim scurried towards the door, Djamila being taken along.

"Why are we going in here?" Djamila inquired.

"Let's see if the above is vacant," he replied.

They ascended the stairwell, to the second floor. A corridor lay to the left. Moving along the corridor, the first room to their right revealed a door wide open. Karim proceeded with caution, soon discovering that not only was the room vacant, but the French doors that led to the balcony were wide open as well. He released his grip from her hand, and moved straight to the balcony, overlooking Rue Charles Péguy. The view gave Karim an overhead shot of the turmoil that unfolded—fists being thrown, police swinging their batons, cries for calm and to restore order from others. Meanwhile, Djamila stood by in the room, well behind Karim. This was Karim's moment to seize, and call out to those of Algerian descent who had gathered—which unavoidably would be heard by the masses of Europeans on hand as well—, and *that* he did, in a volume of voice loud enough to be heard by all, proclaiming: "*To my fellow Algerians–*"

Time seemed to have frozen. The throng looked to have simultaneously paused from the disorder, shifting their eyes above to the voice calling out from the balcony. Karim was met with a swift interjection from Djamila. "Karim, what do you think you're doing? Get away from there!" she said.

Not saying a word nor turning around to face her, Karim extended his right arm, his hand in a 'stop' motion; a non-verbal *please be quiet* gesture. He continued:

We have achieved a glorious victory; one that is unprecedented. One hundred thirty-two years in the making. A great destiny awaits us. We are claiming what is ours; what rightfully belongs to us. Gaining our sovereignty and rights are imminent–

"Karim, I hear footsteps from the back. Someone is coming," a worrisome voice from Djamila.

Karim resumed: "*Our time has come! Vive l'Algérie!*"

Right after, a gunshot was fired in Karim's direction; a bullet landing at the top of the door frame behind him, thereby missing him. Startled, and unable to tell who fired the shot nor which direction the shot came from, Karim turned around and dashed back into the room.

"Let's get out of here!" he said.

"We can't go back out there now?"

"Perhaps there's a rear exit somewhere?" Karim responded. "Or let's find someplace else to hide in this building for now."

Karim took the lead, with Djamila right behind him,

and just after passing the doorway, a man who was hiding behind the wall had emerged and clubbed Karim smack on the left side of his head with a large vase! The impact was so strong, causing Karim to fall to the ground. Djamila let out a frantic scream, terrified at the brutal assault. The man, a European, stocky, well built and above six feet in height, took off immediately on foot, descending the staircase.

Djamila rushed to Karim's aid, getting down to her knees, away from the shards of porcelain scattered on the floor, to take a closer look at the left side of his head. Blood was gushing out. Karim was in deep pain, didn't say one word, but wasn't unconscious. "Oh my, you're badly wounded," Djamila said. She had nothing on hand, not even a headscarf to which she could use to wipe off the blood from his head. "Karim, can you hear me? Answer me," she added.

He gave a nod of his head, uttering a monosyllable response of "yes."

"Listen, you need medical attention right away. We can't stay, so let's get out of here. More trouble could be on the way if we stick around any longer," Djamila said.

Another gunshot was heard, through the balcony. "C'mon, I'll help you up. On your feet," she said. Clutching both upper arms, Djamila aided Karim to his feet, blood still trickling down his face and drops landing on his shirt and pants. Djamila then locked arms with Karim to get a firm hold of him. They descended the staircase, and through the main entrance door.

Outside, chaos had erupted. Several gunshots could be heard, though Djamila couldn't tell from which direction. Karim was hunched over, with Djamila tending to him. "We've got to get to the car right away!" she exclaimed. She then put her right arm over his hunched back, as a way to help shield him from being struck by a passing bullet. The two hurried to the car, scurrying up the street, then turning the corner, soon arriving safely to the vehicle without any further harm done.

"Give me the key," she said. Karim pulled out the key from his pocket, only to fumble it, landing on the ground. Djamila bent down to reach for it off the ground, and then opened the back door in haste to allow Karim to get in. He immediately lay on his side in the backseat. Once behind the wheel, Djamila frantically took off.

"Take me to the hospital," Karim muttered, though still audible enough for Djamila to hear.

Djamila didn't respond, but in her mind, the answer was *no*. She had no intention of taking him to the hospital. Reflecting on the events that had just transpired, she had a hunch–*I don't have a good feeling about it*–, convinced that there would be a *ratonnade* for Karim at the hospital should she take him there, so it was best to take him elsewhere, in a private place.

Djamila turned onto Avenue Pasteur, and a foolish pedestrian attempted to jaywalk the street right in front of the car, causing her to slam on the brakes and honk the horn a few times, only agitating her more. She then sped up the street and into the Tunnel des Facultés, where she nearly grazed a taxi to the right of her. Unfazed by the rather reckless driving, Djamila persisted, eager to get home as quickly as possible.

She arrived at Rue Adolphe Blasselle, parking the car only feet away from the apartment. Exiting the vehicle, Djamila assisted Karim to get out, her arm locked with his, slowly leading him up the staircase. She opened the door and they entered the apartment, both of them finally confined in a safe, private space, away from the outside world.

Straight to the bathroom, Karim closed the toilet lid and took a seat as Djamila went to retrieve a clean, damp cloth. He tilted his head back, seeming fatigued, in addition to his wounds, and was soon handed the cloth.

"So you're not...going to take me to the hospital?" he asked.

"Karim, have you forgotten that I'm a nurse?"

As if he had experienced a 'brain freeze,' seemingly losing sight, or rather memory, of who Djamila was. "Yes, it seems I did. My mistake," he replied.

"Let me take care of you." Taking hold of both hands, she helped pull Karim up, off the closed toilet seat, and moved him to the mirror. Seeing his reflection, he washed his hands and with the damp cloth, took one gentle stroke after another in wiping the blood off his face. The wounds were located on the left cheek, and up to the forehead, with one just above the eyebrow and another a rather large, deep one, right below the hairline, marring his face. Meanwhile, Djamila turned on the shower, adjusting the knob for the cold water; a stream of water shooting out of the showerhead.

"Come rinse your face. No soap," she said, and then moved him to the shower. Karim, without stepping into the shower, leaned forward, rinsing his face as traces of remaining blood landed on the shower's floor, all the while being careful not to get his clothes wet as no spare men's clothing was available. He turned off the shower and was handed another clean, but dry cloth by Djamila to dry off his face. Afterwards, Djamila led Karim to her bedroom, getting him to lie on the bed, flat on his back, even taking off his shoes.

Djamila then went to the medicine cabinet in the bathroom. She always kept an abundance of medical supplies on hand at home, which were to be taken with her on the road when she had to treat wounded ALN soldiers, most often out in the rural areas. A sure sign of how prepared she was; how much she took her nursing duties seriously, and perhaps, another reason as to why she felt that Karim would receive medical attention much quicker at her apartment than had she taken him to the hospital.

She returned to Karim. "Don't touch your wounds," Djamila said, putting on a pair of surgical gloves. "I'm going to apply some antibiotic ointment." Reaching for the tube, she began to apply a thin layer of ointment over each wound. Karim flinched as a result of the ointment making skin contact, wincing momentarily, but the irritation dissipated. Otherwise, he lay still in the bed, as if it was his own mother treating him. "After a while, I'll put some bandages over it," Djamila added.

"Thanks for coming to my aid and for treating me," Karim said.

"I wasn't going to abandon you and leave you alone."

"That's what good friends are for, and you demonstrated that."

"Now whether I supported your actions is another story. But nevertheless, you don't turn your back on someone who is close to you."

"Well, that's the risk I took. But I'll be fine. I'll overcome this in no time."

"In the name of God, amen."

Djamila stepped away for a bit and returned, bringing him a tall glass of water. Karim sat up on the bed and leaned his back against the headboard, and finished the glass in no time. Djamila then reached for the box of adhesive bandages on the bedside table and placed a bandage over each of Karim's facial wounds. "Get some rest. I'll let you be and will check on you later," she said.

Karim nodded his head, and before long, fell into a doze.

Some three hours had passed. During that time, Djamila had a tea pot on the stove, brewing some mint tea, as well as preparing a *karantika*–a dish resembling a kind of savory pancake, made of chickpea flour–baked in a casserole dish. In checking on Karim again, she returned to the bedroom with a tray carrying a glass of tea and a small plate featuring a good portion of *karantika*. Karim was awake, having had plenty of rest.

"*Ça va mieux?*" Djamila asked, setting the tray on the bedside table. *Feeling better?*

"Yeah, I would say so," Karim answered.

"Here, eat something." She brought the plate to him and Karim sat up, taking hold of the plate. Breaking a piece off with the fork, he consumed a good piece of the *karantika*–light, fluffy, and moist.

"Delicious. You sure have that cooking touch as well," Karim said.

"It's a recipe that was shared with me by a *fatma* some time ago."

"Perhaps I shouldn't be telling you this, but you caring for me, I can't help but to think that it reminds me of my mother."

"Oh, how kind of you to say, Karim."

Karim took another huge bite of the *karantika*, and washed it down with a gulp of the mint tea. He then rose out of bed and went to the bathroom to check on his wounds.

Partially peeling off one of the bandages, the ointment had settled into the wound, well into the process of healing the wound. A look at another wound above the eyebrow revealed the same. Karim washed his hands and walked out of the bathroom, met by Djamila. He stood in front of her, and took hold of her left hand, and then her right, meeting her eyes. She looked almost thunderstruck, perhaps intimidated to an extent, but Karim was determined to be steadfast and direct in the message he wanted to convey to her.

"Djamila, I want you to know that I'm glad that you're in my life," he said.

"Me too, Karim. I feel the same way," Djamila replied. "But what are you trying to get at here?"

He took a deep swallow and said, "I want us to be together."

"You're not saying this because of me helping you?"

Karim shook his head. "No." He continued, "Since the first time I saw you, I've had an affection for you. But moreover, that day you accompanied me at *L'Écho d'Alger* with the chic disguise you had on, you looked like one of the most stunning women I had ever laid my eyes upon. It's something that's been etched in my mind ever since. Sure, I understand it was merely a disguise, but nevertheless, my feelings towards you are the same. Beyond that, I've come to know the woman you are–caring, compassionate, gentle, and a heart of gold."

"Wow," she uttered, "never has a man told me this."

Karim pulled her in closer, and gave her a light kiss on the cheek. Djamila said nothing, yet willingly chose to reciprocate, putting her arms around Karim, and kissing him on his right cheek, avoiding the bandage-covered wounds on the other cheek. Karim delighted–on the inside, suppressing any outwardly expression–in the fact that the feeling was mutual.

"In the midst of the turmoil going on in the city, let's get out of town for a while. It's for the best, I think," Karim said.

"Sure, let's do."

"Anything you wish to take with you, let's put it in the car."

Djamila found it necessary to inform her parents in writing of her leaving town, in large part because she had no idea how long she would be away from Algiers nor where she'd be going to with Karim. Rather than bombard Karim with questions of *where and for how long*, she allowed Karim to take charge and lead, in an act of submission. Tearing off a piece of paper from a notepad and a pen in hand, Djamila wrote a simple note of: *Mama/Papa, I'm heading out of town with Karim. Don't know when I'll be back home, but I'll be fine. Love, Djamila*. She then left the note on the dining table.

The two of them wasted little time in leaving the apartment, heading down the staircase and into the car. Karim took caution in choosing the route to take, completely avoiding Bab-el-Oued. Helicopters and fighter planes hovered above, an undeniable sign of the chaos taking place on the streets of Bab-el-Oued. He said nothing to Djamila as far as the destination he had in mind. They drove by a number of buildings whose walls had been daubed by graffiti that featured OAS propaganda. In due time, Karim headed up the road that led to the lot of the Notre Dame d'Afrique, the famed Catholic church of the city, arriving before dusk.

The car parked, both exited the vehicle and moved towards the balustrade railing that partly enclosed the church grounds. Djamila focused above, at the sky; helicopters and fighter planes in rather close distance. "Karim, you seem to be attracted to action and chaos and not want to be far from it," she said.

Karim appeared to have taken offense at the remark. "We won't be here long, I can assure you. Maybe just fifteen–"

"I'm just kidding with you," Djamila replied, cutting him off and also putting a hand on his forearm, displaying affection.

Her clarification and physical touching calmed him. "Not to make light of what we're seeing in the distance, but surely we're out of harm's way."

The two moved closer to each other, leaning against the balustrade railing, taking in the spectacular view of not only the city itself, but also the Bay of Algiers and beyond–the Mediterranean Sea. Ships were seen docked at the bay, as well as a sailboat out at sea.

"So beautiful, this view. Breathtaking, really. One can easily see why the French have been determined in preserving colonial Algeria," she said.

Karim put his arm around her waist. "No doubt, when the French first laid eyes upon our beautiful land and coast, they were enthralled by it," Karim replied. He turned his head to face her. "Don't tell me this is your first time here?"

"Of course not. But I've only been here on a few occasions, because, you know, what's behind us." A not so subtle clue, *the Catholic church.*

"Why yes, the church."

"But perhaps I should stop by more often solely for the view alone." Djamila followed by putting her right arm around Karim's waist, the two of them now tugging each other at the waist. "It makes me wonder, how much longer will there be conflict over there? What do you think?"

"Well, beyond today, that's for sure. I wouldn't have the slightest idea for how long though, but I see this as a good sign."

"A positive sign?"

"Well yes, when have we seen something like this? The army, the government reining in the diehard, pro-French Algeria cult? Even those in authority, in positions of power, whose duty is to maintain law and order–or, as we've seen recently, attempt to *restore* law and order, rather–, surely they're so fed up with the OAS and their agitators."

"Well said."

Karim and Djamila turned around and headed back to the car. They drove off, pleased to leave the tumult of town and commence a getaway.

V

Karim and Djamila spent close to a week in Arzew, a port town near Oran in western Algeria, a first for Karim in venturing to this part of the country. An *escapade* that consisted of basking under the sun at the beach, strolling along the sand, ascending atop coastal hills, and indulging in bomb *glaces* at the town center. Both respected the nature of their relationship, sleeping in separate beds in the hotel room as they were not a married couple.

An admission was made by the hotel proprietor that he was firm on his decision to "close shop within a month and move to France." Karim sensed that there were no bitter, hard feelings by the proprietor towards either the de Gaulle-led government nor the Algerian nationalists. But rather, a frank acknowledgement that "in just the past week since the signing of the Évian Accords, I've noticed a sharp drop in clientele. I suspect it will only get worse from here on out. Not to mention fears for our safety and well-being; that is, being met with reprisals. The writing is on the wall, and it's best for me and my family to move on."

April 1. On returning to Algiers, Karim learned of the news that a horde of Algerians descending Rue de Lyon in a procession were fatally run down by an enraged driver, only a stone's throw away from a Muslim cemetery. Some two dozen Algerians were killed. Moreover, he learned that a handful of the procession's participants later caught up to the driver at an intersection, and managed to successfully pull the driver out of the vehicle and fatally beat him. *At least some justice was served.*

As a result of this incident, Karim sought to provide any sort of aid to his fellow Algerians in the form of firearms for defense, first and foremost. He hadn't paid a visit to Amandine in a long time, and was eager to find out what firearms she might have stored in her place of business. Fearing the random, or targeted, pedestrian attack, Karim opted to drive to the tailor shop. Arriving and then parking on Rue Rovigo on a lovely, sunny afternoon, he noticed the glass door to the tailor shop was wide open.

Amandine was sitting on a wooden chair just behind the counter and jumped up out of her seat at the sight of Karim.

"Karim, where have you been? I haven't seen you in ages, it seems," she said.

"Operating in the shadows. Here and there," Karim replied. "I'm pleased to see you again. You look to be doing fine, safe and sound, in the midst of all the chaos around the city."

"Staying safe, yes. I'm doing my part."

"Listen, going back to last year, Sofiane had intentions

of storing weapons here, but he later decided not to, transporting the weapons instead to the east, as far as I know. Since then, did he ever stop by here to store any, without my knowledge?"

"He did stop by. Just once, in fact," Amandine answered.

"So he did?"

"I want to say back around October?" She added, "But only handguns, he told me."

"Handguns, that's it? Not even any grenades, bombs, rifles?"

"Correct, according to him."

Karim still had to wrap his head around the response. "How strange. Let me take a look at them. In the same storage space I recall, right?"

"Same place."

Amandine led him to the back. The floor and surroundings were much more cleaner and maintained than the last time Karim recalled–minimal clutter about, with regards to pieces of cut up yarn and other material waste from clothing. She introduced one of her employees, Rachid, sitting behind a desk laboring away at a sewing machine, before dismissing him for a half-hour break so as to not have him discover the storage space and the contents of it.

"Sofiane shared with me a story of how he was on his way home and was surprised to see that the *flics* surrounded his apartment building. Knowing he had firearms in his trunk, he took off promptly to avoid running into the police, and needed a place to unload the guns. That's when he stopped by and asked me if he could hide the guns here, to which I allowed him to," Amandine said to Karim.

"Interesting, I must say," he replied.

"And I haven't seen nor heard from him since."

Amandine then retrieved a key ring and flashlight from her office, followed by leading Karim to the storage space, unlocking the padlock that secured the door. Karim swung the door wide open, and, flashlight in hand, went inside. A dingy place, he moved the light around and it didn't take long for him to spot an assortment of handguns. Karim counted some twenty or so–two Berettas, a few revolvers, and other pistols. He stepped out for a moment, Amandine idling at the door.

"Do you have a sack? Something sturdy that I can put the guns in," he asked.

"I believe I do," Amandine replied. She went to retrieve one, which turned out to be exactly what Karim was looking for, bearing a striking resemblance to a burlap bag, and handed it to him. "I don't touch guns," she remarked, her hands up in a kind of capitulation gesture, "I'll leave it all to you."

Karim reentered the space and inspected a handgun to see if it was loaded, dislodging the magazine. He reached for another, and then the next one, which was a revolver, fully loaded. Yet, he counted eight firearms without any bullets.

One by one, Karim placed the guns into the bag, making sure that all ammunition was unloaded to prevent the accidental discharge. After, he exited the storage space once more.

"I'm only going to take half of the firearms with me," Karim said to Amandine.

"Oh why? You don't want them all?" she replied.

"If Sofiane were to return and discover that all the firearms are gone, he'll know that it was I who took them. By only taking a select number, it won't look so obvious and will suppress any anger from him. Him and I are not on good terms."

"Understood, and I won't question it any further. As you say."

Amandine closed the storage door shut, securing it with the padlock. The two then moved towards the front of the shop.

"So how's business going?" Karim asked.

"Oh, lately we've been experiencing a slight dip in revenue," she replied.

"How slight?"

"Ten percent, give or take, according to my bookkeeper, who keeps me in the loop once per week regarding finances."

"And you expect it to get worse?" he asked. A rhetorical question, of course, but Karim sought to get Amandine to reveal as much information as possible.

She nodded her head. "No doubt about it. And you want to know something? Throughout the time that I have supported the FLN cause, I have always questioned my future here. Should I stay in or leave Algeria? And if I stay, for how much longer? But now, with the Évian Accords a done deal, some well-off clients of mine have already left, resulting in less business for me. In addition to there being no prospect of dual citizenship, I have therefore made the decision that I will be leaving Algeria."

"The line in the sand has been drawn, as far as citizenship goes."

"That's the reality of it."

"I'd like to think that you have options, in terms of where to go to."

Amandine sighed. "In short, yes. But, we already left France before, so I ask myself, 'Why go back?' Yet, I do suspect many fellow Jews will make that decision to relocate there, and for good reasons. Based on what I've been hearing through word of mouth, that's exactly where many Jews are heading to."

"You have a lot to ponder about, and do."

"More than ever. I'm leaning towards California. Los Angeles to be more precise, and setting up shop there where I would have access and exposure to the immense entertainment industry."

"Wow, the United States. It must be the dream of any capitalist, any ambitious person seeking prosperity. Well, what little I have heard about it, anyway."

"Right you are, Karim."

"Well, if we don't see each other again, may I wish you safety, good health and prosperity."

"Same to you, young man. You deserve it."

Karim headed out, carrying the burlap bag with the firearms inside, carefully waiting for the opportune time to hurry straight to his car so as to prevent any arousal of suspicion from pedestrians, before getting behind the wheel and driving off.

Noureddine gained temporary employment at a construction site in the suburb of Hydra, delighted to return to his usual trade as a bricklayer. The assignment was to last until the end of June, with the possibility of it being extended "depending on the present state of the Algérois economy" as he was told, in light of the ongoing exodus of Europeans from the city. Noureddine requested to borrow some money–"about a week's worth of expenses"–from Karim, to which Karim agreed to accommodate him.

After filling up the gas tank at a Shell *station-service*

in Telemly, Karim was on his way to meet Noureddine. A gorgeous spring day, one reminiscent of summer, perfect for being away from the indoor confines and spending time outside. Traveling along, he spotted five teenagers, all boys, walking up the road, sporting white *djellabas*. Nothing appeared to be out of the ordinary.

Continuing on his drive, about a third of a kilometer later, an odd noise sprung from the car, emanating from the rear, it seemed. Karim guessed the sound to be that coming from one of the tires. Right away, he pulled over to the side of the road, safe from the oncoming traffic. He got out of the car to take a look around and sure enough, he discovered a popped tire on the rear, right side. Pointless to call out for any help, he thought, as not one pedestrian, not one passerby was in sight at that time, Karim went ahead to open the trunk and lifted up the trunk board. To his relief, he found a spare tire, as well as a black iron 4-way lug wrench, the ideal tool for removing the bolts from the tire. One mighty turn clockwise of the handle yielded nothing. Another try, and the same result. The bolts were tightly secured, and Karim realized it was going to be a struggle to unloosen them.

The same group of teenage boys who Karim spotted down the road earlier were now crossing his path. Seeing the struggle that Karim was experiencing, one of the boys approached him and asked, "Need any help, sir?"

"Nah, I should be fine here. But thanks anyway," Karim replied.

The boys resumed their walk, and Karim gave it another go with the lug wrench. Still unsuccessful at removing even one of the bolts, frustration overwhelmed him. "Fuck," he said to himself. He then turned to look ahead, farther up the road where the boys were. "Hey!" Karim shouted, to which the boys heard the call, and turned around. "On second thought, I could use some help," he said. "These damn bolts are secured tight and I can't get them off. Can one of you get a firm grip on this other handle and turn it clockwise?"

One boy, who looked more well built than the others, with a noticeable scar on his right wrist as the *djellaba's* sleeve did not overlap it, took the lead. Gripping another handle, the boy exerted all his might, grunting in the process, to turn the lug wrench. Success! The lug wrench made a full 360-degree turn, and then another. And another. The first bolt was unloosened. In succession, they managed to remove the other three bolts. Karim retrieved the spare tire from the trunk and installed it in no time.

"That should do it. Thanks for your help. Much appreciated," Karim said. His extended hand was met with a soft squeeze. "You boys be careful out there. Chaos and violence seem to be spreading like wildfire in town."

"We're well aware of it. We learned just this morning of an explosion that occurred down the street at a rug factory," one of the other boys said, thick eyebrows, a butch cut, who looked to be no older than fourteen perhaps. He gave his name, which was Younes.

"Really?"

"Yes, we had to take a walk down there and see the damage for ourselves. The owner of the factory frequents our *boucherie*, so we know him. We've no idea if he perished or is still alive."

Ah, a man who frequents a Halal butcher shop. "So it was an Algerian man whose business was targeted?" Karim said.

Younes nodded his head.

"I'd like to know the man's name, if you don't mind."

"Sure, I can tell you. His name is Nassim Mokrani."

Karim repeated the name as confirmation.

"Since you're asking, why is it of interest to you?"

"You need not have any fear of me; don't worry, I'm no law enforcement official. I'm fighting the good fight for our people, to gain our independence from the colonizer. But moreover, I'm an information gatherer."

"Good to hear, sir."

If this man was killed in the explosion, was he purposely targeted by the OAS, or by the FLN for being a possible traitor, a harki? Karim wondered. "Know anything about where he stood in terms of this ongoing conflict?" he asked, speaking about the owner in the past tense in assuming that the man was killed. "Was he supportive of the FLN, or possibly a traitor who sympathized with the enemy?"

"Oh no, no. He supported the FLN and the independence movement. Sure, he may have sold rugs to the Europeans to line his own pockets, but he was on our side in support of Algerian independence."

"Understood then. I've something I want to show you." Karim went to the trunk once more, this time bringing out the burlap bag. Another bag, a much smaller one, was also inside, which carried the ammunition. He then opened the passenger's door and sat down, but facing the boys, his feet resting on the road pavement. He called the boys to move closer. Karim looked around, making sure no one else was in sight, and pulled out a Beretta, along with its magazine from both bags. "Have any of you ever used a firearm?" he asked them.

All five boys turned to look at one another, mouths agape in astonishment, in coming within arm's reach of a handgun. They shook their heads and answered "No." The boys' eyes were gazed on the weapon like a baby fixated on a toy.

"Let me give you a brief tutorial," he said. Karim, scanning his eyes around him once more, up and down the road, and behind him as well, followed with proper gun safety protocols and overall gunhandling, including loading bullets into the magazine and inserting the magazine into the Beretta, and subsequently, inserting bullets into the cylinder of a revolver. The boys seemed to catch on.

"It's for your protection," Karim went on, "God knows what turmoil will unfold moving forward. Will you take them?"

Younes looked to the boy to his left, then to the other boys to his right. He nodded. "Yes, we'll take them. They may come in handy."

"In ordinary circumstances, I might think twice about furnishing firearms to minors, knowing I'd be locked up if caught. But in times like this, no time for regrets." Karim placed the revolver, along with the bullets back in the burlap bag, and handed it to Younes. "Oh, if anyone asks who gave this to you, just say it was some stranger. Don't leave any hint that it was from me."

"You got it, sir."

"Is the butcher shop far from here? Let me give you a ride there. Might not be a good idea carrying *that* around, if the walk is far."

"We have a ways to walk, but we won't all fit in the car. Here, take the bag, and meet us at Boucherie Moussa."

In due course, parked curbside in front of the butcher shop, Karim handed the burlap bag containing the firearms and ammunition to Younes again. "Hey, I'm here to help. If you ever need to find me, head over to the Upper Casbah.

Ask for Karim B., and any resident will guide you to me,"
Karim said.

"I'll keep that in mind, thanks," Younes replied.

"I'm with the FLN, so you know."

"Much respect to you, sir."

Karim invited Djamila to his apartment for a gathering. But more specifically, for the purpose of introducing her to his mother. She arrived at eleven in the morning. Right away, from the moment Djamila entered the apartment, Sara took an immediate liking to Djamila, Karim sensed. Political talk was kept to a minimum, with more focus and emphasis on the two women getting to know each other. Ever helpful in the kitchen, Djamila assisted in chopping several vegetables, preparing a Tunisian salad made from jarred tuna, boiled potatoes, parsley, olives and a hearty dollop of harissa–a recipe she picked up during time spent in Tunisia. All served with a basket of *kesra*. At dusk, Karim gave her a tour of the Casbah, leading her through the maze-like streets, and they then ascended to a rooftop, overlooking the city and sea. At the end of the night, following Djamila's departure, Sara dropped the hint to her son that "she's the right woman for you." Karim read the exact meaning of her remark without a second thought, though suppressing his expressions.

April 19. He already started envisioning a wedding day to come, despite having yet made a marriage proposal to Djamila. Premature without a doubt, but the thought of what attire Karim would wear on such a day encouraged him to want to start looking, at the very least. One obstacle for him though: Karim pretty much depleted all the funds he'd received back in West Germany. He knew that in the not-too-distant future, he would be back to being a penniless teenager, but this was not enough to discourage him and send him into a state of gloom and depression. Even when he'd have thoughts of, *oh how I wish I was still collecting monthly remuneration from Sofiane*, Karim nevertheless managed to maintain a positive outlook.

The haberdashery owned by the Béroujon family was the right place to stop by. A lovely, sunny April day, Bab-el-Oued carried a different atmosphere and feeling–residents who looked confused, agitated, acting in more of a haste than usual. Some French flags were still draped over the balconies of apartments by those who apparently were holding out hope that there would be some sort of reversal or nullification of the Évian Accords, thereby preserving Algeria under French colonial rule. Karim worried even more so for his own safety, and upon parking the car on Avenue Durando, he wasted no time in heading straight into the store. He spotted Madame Béroujon towards the back, near the tuxedo section, carelessly tossing a set of folded dress shirts onto a clothing display table, likely out of frustration or anger, shouting something to a person farther in the rear, possibly her husband. Karim took a few steps forward, waiting for Madame Béroujon to turn to face him and meet his eyes.

"I'm sorry, Madame. Did I catch you at a bad time?" he asked.

She didn't respond right away, instead focusing on him, giving the typical look of appraisal. "No. It's never the wrong time for a customer," she replied.

"You remember me, right?"

"Your face rings a bell. Remind me your name again?"

"Karim."

"Yes, now I recall. Frustrations are mounting for us. Business has been bad lately. We're going under, it seems."

"Sorry to hear that."

"Well, our days are numbered. We're on our way out, soon...not *if*, but *when*."

"I've spoken to others who've shared the same sentiment."

"My husband and I, we also own another business, outside of town. Being at a crossroads, I ask my husband, 'Are we under a delusion that we'd be able to retain anything of what's left of our assets, or come to terms and accept the reality that we're about to lose everything?' This is a nightmare." She paused as if to momentarily reflect, and continued, "Well, you're here, to shop of course. So what can I do for you?"

"I'd like to have a look at your tuxedos and slacks."

She led Karim towards the rear of the store, straight to the section displaying the tuxedos. Sharp, clean-cut, perfect for the occasion. *But*, was he going to actually wear one, or a traditional Algerian outfit for his dream day he hoped would come? Karim had yet to make a decision of course, and one that wouldn't come anytime soon.

"I'll give you a huge discount if you take it now. Forty percent off the retail price," Madame Béroujon said.

"Wow, that's mighty generous of you, Madame. However, as a young Algerian, I have yet to decide if I want to go with a tuxedo or the traditional Islamic garb for a wedding day I envision will come in the near future. I came here just to look."

"Oh, I see...but you do like it?"

"I love it. What's there not to like? It's outstanding! But sorry I won't be walking out with it at this time."

"Understood."

"But otherwise, although it's no concern of mine regarding your business affairs, but a good friend of mine is a lawyer. He has a close contact who is an accountant, but also, if I'm not mistaken, is some kind of financial advisor as well. Don't quote me on the exact title. Perhaps this man may be of service to you and your husband. Interested?"

Madame lit up with relief. "Oh, that would be wonderful, Karim. I welcome any help that we can get."

"Great. Go see the lawyer. He's a Spaniard, a standout professional, and he's here in Bab-el-Oued." Karim reached into his wallet, hoping he still kept Sebastián's business card tucked inside. Sure enough, he retrieved it. "He's an influential figure in town, by way of utilizing political connections and word of mouth," Karim added, before kindly handing the business card to Madame Béroujon. "His name is Sebastián."

"Ah, yes. Now I know who you're speaking of."

"Mention that I sent you to him."

"Will do. Thank you, young man."

"Sorry I didn't make a purchase from you today. Should I return, you can rest assured I'll be taking the tuxedo and slacks."

"If I'm still here."

Karim left the haberdashery and got in the car, driving just a short distance and parking as close as possible to Sebastián's law office to prevent any chance of encountering a sudden outburst of violence by any passerbys. Ascending the stairwell as usual, Karim knocked on the door and was greeted by Mathilde, who led him into Sebastián's office.

There Sebastián sat, comfy in his plush, leather executive chair, leaning back, feet kicked up atop the desk.

"Relaxing?" Karim asked.

"I guess you can say that. Client visits have dwindled in number lately, and of course I won't just lounge at home during the day, so I do it here," Sebastián answered.

Karim took a seat. "But at least you're not struggling and facing dire straits with finances, am I correct?"

"You're right." Sebastián nodded his head. "Even now, I'm doing fine. Let's face it, as a lawyer, I'm not poor."

"I noticed in the main reception area, there's less paperwork, stationery and adornments."

"We're cleaning house, and the reason is obvious. Clarisse, the paralegal, already said goodbye to us, packing her bags and leaving Algeria, and following suit will be Mathilde."

"Listen, I have a request to make, and I know I'm going to sound like I'm making a plea, and, dare I say it–sound like a beggar, if you will–but first I should mention that I intend to propose marriage to a woman named Djamila–"

"Ah, you're looking to get married? Good for you, Karim."

"But, as you may know, I don't have a job, so I'm turning to you to inquire and seek about any employment you, or someone you know, may be able to offer me as a means of being able to provide financially, in what I hope will soon result in marriage for me."

"Oh, that's more than fair to ask. Why did I get the impression at first that your request would be in regards to some dire situation you're facing?"

Karim shrugged his shoulders. "Perhaps it came across as such. Just the mere giving of something without receiving anything in return is typically frowned upon and met with a 'no' response these days. And in general, I hate having to beg people for anything."

"Same here, my friend."

"It'd be a much different story approaching my mom, other family members, someone who I share a bloodline with, as opposed to someone I'm not related to."

"Well, you're no stranger to me, Karim. And we've been acquainted for about a year now, if my memory serves me correctly." Sebastián paused for a moment, and resumed, "So here's the deal; my situation as it stands: I'm leaving Algeria soon, permanently. You're aware that we're heading back to Spain for retirement, and the current political and social climate justifies this as the right timing for us. I'm in the process of consolidating my business, assets, and personal belongings. There's not a whole lot I can suggest to you at this time, but that can change at any moment. Do know, any formal employment–that is, not one in which you're earning cash 'under the table'–that you were to obtain right now, whilst still under French colonial rule, could immediately turn upside down once Algeria is officially declared an independent state."

"Of course, which doesn't work in my favor. And which is why I seem to be under the belief that I should seek employment with a company run by Algerians."

"However, what I can say to you is this: First off, you did meet up with Sami the lawyer when you stayed in Paris, just to confirm?"

"Yes."

"Well, I spoke to him a week ago and he stated, or *confirmed* I should say, that in light of the Évian Accords, he will be moving back to Algiers in the summer, and will be joining a boutique law firm comprised solely of Algerians. It had been brought to my attention that the firm is seeking both a mail clerk and a typist. Sounds like something that piques your interest?"

"Oh, yes. Absolutely!" Karim responded with excitement.

"Nothing was mentioned though in regards to remuneration," Sebastián admitted.

"Remuneration can be discussed at a later time. The most important thing for me is to actually secure employment first."

"Indeed. I'll put in a good word and recommend you for the role."

"Many thanks. This brings me much delight, hearing this news."

"My pleasure. By the way, how was your working relationship with Sami back in Paris?"

"Great, as far as I'm concerned. We got along quite well and established solid rapport in working together. In fact, he treated me more like a brother, which bodes well should I indeed end up working with him again. He spoke of his desire to return to Algeria someday."

"And that desire will soon come to fruition."

"Oh, before I arrived here, I spoke to a businesswoman who, along with her husband, own a haberdashery. She told me they are closing shop, as many are, and they're in great need for financial advice. I suggested to her to reach out to you, as I know you have contacts who specialize in that domain of finances and such. Expect a visit or call from a Madame and/or Monsieur Béroujon. Marie-Hélène and Frédéric Béroujon."

"Ah, so a mom-and-pop shop?"

"Yes. I know, *small fish* compared to your usual clients and connections."

"Oh no no, not at all. I welcome them. Another client

who needs help during these tumultuous times. Hey, you've done favors for me, and you can count on me to repay you. I'll do my part to see that you'll have a good, stable job soon."

"*Muchas gracias, señor.* You know, it must be said though, on my part, when I pay you visits to chat and ask for favors, it's just that I don't have a father around to lean on, so I feel I need to turn to another grown adult male figure for guidance; for wisdom."

"No apology needed, Karim. It's all well understood. The best of luck to you in your coming marriage proposal. May it be the result you've been wishing for."

A man goes after what he wants in life, Karim recalled, out of the blue, something his father once said. What did it matter, that perhaps he didn't understand the full picture of it at the time, at a still-adolescent age? *Ah, that's what I needed to spring into mind,* Karim thought. He walked out his apartment, standing tall, resolute in his convictions and state of mind. A spontaneous eruption of violence involving some twenty or so people broke out on Rue Charles Aboulker, to which Karim turned around and left immediately to avoid being caught in the middle of it. He eventually arrived at Djamila's apartment, knocking on the door, to which she responded promptly, welcoming him in.

An ironboard assembled in the living room, Djamila had been in the middle of ironing clothing–a sizeable quantity ahead of her to take care of. "You've come at the right time, Karim. Make yourself useful. Everything you see on the sofa has just been ironed. Kindly fold the towels and the clothes, save for the women's clothing. Leave that for me," she instructed him.

Karim took a look at the clothes on the sofa before touching anything. "Your weekly ironing routine?" he asked.

She nodded her head, a slight grin. "Yes. I couldn't see myself doing this every day, not even if it was just one item of clothing. Not to mention, I'm not home every day, as you already know." What she referred to as "women's clothing" consisted of a coffee-colored blouse, khakis and a headscarf–all moved aside by Karim.

"You never seem to be in a sour mood," Karim said.

Djamila looked as if she had to think hard about his remark. "Yeah, hardly ever, really. My outlook on life remains pretty consistent."

Karim neatly folded eight towels, including two kitchen rags, and set them on a large, long rectangular wicker basket with double handles.

"I must say, it was a pleasure meeting and getting to know your mother. She's done well in raising you. *That* is evident," she said.

"Kind of you to say, Djamila. Being the widow that she is, my mother has big shoes to fill. An enormous burden on her, to say the least, not to mention four children in total," Karim replied. "A father is irreplaceable."

Djamila dipped her head in acknowledgement. "I know. I'm thankful to still have mine."

"Would I have ever joined the FLN if my father was still around? Who knows? But I would be under his direction and tutelage, without question. He'd probably recoil in horror at the mere thought of his son dropping out of high school."

"Good point."

Djamila wrapped up the last of her ironing, passing the clothing over to Karim to fold. "Well, my work is done," she said. Djamila then moved to the French door that led to the balcony. As she swung the curtain over to the left, Karim approached her. He then wrapped his left arm around her waist, to which she turned to face him, and he pulled her in closer.

"Djamila, there's something I've been meaning to tell you, and in doing so, to just keep it short and get straight to the point." He paused for a few seconds and continued, "I so much enjoy spending time with you. To think how we met as associates, as colleagues, in this pursuit of fighting for our independence from colonial rule, up until the present, we've certainly had our share of unique and interesting moments together. And may it not end there. May it continue. In working with you and getting to know you better, I want to tell you from the bottom of my heart that I want to be with you. You're the woman I want to do life with." Karim reached into his left pocket and pulled out a 0.5-carat, sterling silver engagement ring that was neither covered nor boxed—one that he could afford as he was given a fifty-percent discount the day prior by a disgruntled European *bijoutier* who settled on taking whatever hard cash Karim offered—and slipped it on Djamila's finger. "Will you marry me?"

"Oh," Djamila uttered in delight. She blushed, and put both hands to her face. Tears of joy trickled down her cheeks. "Yes," she said, adding, "Yes, Karim. I'll marry you."

Djamila embraced him, followed by giving him a kiss on the lips, and Karim reciprocated. A man whose goal of marriage would come to fruition sometime in the near future.

May 10. Sofiane paid a visit to the Casbah, in search of

Karim. Upon knocking on the door of the apartment, he was met with a "Karim's not here" from Sara. Apparently, Sofiane was discreet and rather evasive with regards to the nature of what he wanted to discuss with Karim, but demanded that he speak with Karim "tomorrow." Sara replied in saying, "I'll tell him." Resolute, Sofiane even wrote a note and left it with her to give to Karim, in hopes that it would persuade him to see Sofiane.

"Are you out to harm my son?" she asked, having never met him before, and therefore a bit suspicious of the man.

"Oh no no. Not at all, madame. Have no fear of me," Sofiane answered.

The next morning, Karim awakened, readying himself to go see Sofiane. He viewed the note given to him by his mother, revealing the meeting place: *Jardin d'Essai*, the massive, gorgeous botanical garden located in the El Hamma neighborhood. Karim scooped up a sunny-side-up egg from the skillet with a piece of bread and headed out the door.

Beautiful, clear skies hovered above Algiers, yet the streets were inundated with frustrated Algérois. The trolley buses remained unsafe for residents, and with the destination being somewhat far away, Karim had little to no choice but to catch a taxi to the botanical garden as he no longer had a rental car in his possession. The chauffeur made it a point to keep all the windows rolled up as a precautionary measure while navigating the bustling streets of town, and in doing so, kept the air conditioning on to stay cool inside.

Karim was dropped off at Rue de Lyon, right next to the garden's ticket booth. He purchased a ticket and looked around. No sight of Sofiane, which could only mean that Sofiane was in the garden itself. Entering the garden, Karim then descended the stair steps and arrived at a walkway that led one to other paths, but also straight to the other end of the garden. Palm trees, other beautiful trees and lush greenery abound in this square-shaped botanical garden. Only few visitors were on hand, and farther ahead just off the walkway lay a circular pond. Benches were situated near the pond. Karim then spotted Sofiane, in business casual attire—black slacks, black tennis shoes and a white shirt—standing under the shade of a tree, which made sense—*who would want to sit on a bench under the direct sun for minutes on end while waiting for someone?* Karim took slow steps towards him while Sofiane moved at a quicker pace, approaching him directly.

"Karim, this is long overdue," Sofiane said.

Karim stopped and stood still, motionless. "You know you owe me an apology?" he responded.

Sofiane dipped his head, letting out a sigh. "Yes, I know."

"What you said to me the last time I saw you, I took that as a thinly-veiled threat."

Sofiane raised his head to meet Karim's eyes. "You're exactly right. My actions rubbed you the wrong way, and, I admit it, instilled a sense of fear in you, in spite of all that you've done for me. Not to mention, me acting in my own self-interest. I was in the wrong. Please accept my sincere apologies."

Karim, again, didn't move a muscle before giving a slight nod. "Accepted," he said softly. "But what did you *really* want to see me for?"

"Exactly *that* reason. To acknowledge how wrong I was in my actions towards you and to apologize to you in person."

"Well, it's all in the past now."

"Let's move off the walkway and to the grass," Sofiane said. Once doing so, they were standing under the shade. Sofiane continued, "Look at the progress we've made in being part of the FLN. We are on the verge of officially achieving independence and proclaiming 'mission accomplished.'"

"How sweet that sounds."

"And you yourself played a role in this. I want to personally acknowledge your efforts and contribution, and give credit where credit is due. This is not coming from anyone else within the ranks, but from me personally."

"Well that's pleasing to hear." Karim added, "And where do you go from here?"

"'You mean me specifically?"

"Yes."

"I'll be serving in the coming Algerian government."

"Excellent. You'll be set for a long time then."

"One can only hope. Nothing is a given. There are no guarantees in politics, as far as tenure goes. One day you're sitting nice and comfy in power, and the next day you realize you've been ousted."

"As for me, I'm looking for employment. I'm all but done with being an operative; working 'underground' so to speak. I will only continue to operate in my current capacity until independence is official."

"Am I sensing an interest on your part in seeking to work for the coming Algerian government?"

Karim shrugged. "A possibility. One not to be ruled out. One thing is certain, just to reiterate my previous point: I do not want to accept a job that's clandestine in nature. Those days are all but over. Finding formal employment will be a top priority for me. I am engaged, and I–"

"Congratulations, Karim."

"Thanks," he replied, choosing not to mention to whom–Djamila. "As a soon-to-be married man, it goes without saying that I need to gain employment to provide financially, but I also need to be in a line of work that will keep me out of harm's way."

"Understood." Sofiane motioned to Karim for both of them to move to and proceed down the walkway, in the direction facing the bay. "Listen, in light of our fractured working relationship the past several months, I'd like to give you weekly remuneration–until Algerian independence is officially declared. It's the very least I can do. How does that sound?"

"That would be terrific. I'm pleased to hear that."

"Good. I'm glad we agree. You have my word on it. I'd like to stop by your place this evening and give you your payment. And the next one a week later and so on. Is that OK?"

"That's fine with me."

"And once Algeria is officially an independent nation, let's catch up and assess any interest you may have in pursuing a position with the government. If so, we can discuss it in more detail."

"Sounds like a plan."

In a change of subject, Sofiane said, "The settlers are clearing out, and they surely feel helpless, defenseless, their backs against the wall, with no one to lean on, save for the OAS."

"It brings as much joy to you as it does to me."

"To all of us. This is what we've fought for."

"Have you any idea, even a wild guess, as to when de Gaulle and his government plan on officially recognizing Algeria as a sovereign state? Perhaps you've heard speculation and may be more in the know as an insider, one at the top of the ranks of the FLN."

"My answer to that is: After the OAS officially concedes and ceases to exist as an entity. I know that's not saying much—"

"It isn't."

"But to directly answer the question, no."

"Makes sense. How can we officially be a sovereign state when we have a fringe European minority roaming our streets causing havoc?"

"Exactly. I'd reckon that when their numbers become increasingly insignificant, we'll succeed in delivering the final blow to them; that is, if they don't give in and capitulate by then. But obviously we're not there just yet."

"They're still out for blood."

"Will they give in and acknowledge that their efforts have become futile, or will they self-destruct?"

"*Telle est la question.*"

Sofiane turned to Karim and gave him a hug, to which Karim reciprocated. What had become a sour, fractured working relationship had turned around for the better, to the delight of both men.

May 22. The Algerian vendors who ran their own street market stalls on Rue Randon were fewer in number, almost certainly due to fear of being targeted by disgruntled Europeans, or more specifically the OAS. It was quite noticeable and could not be dismissed as a mere coincidence, not to mention the ongoing exodus itself of Europeans, bringing about a lack of essential services provided throughout the city, and the whole of Algeria for that matter. The result produced a functional breakdown of the city's economy and social life; an undeniable decline in activity. With more and more Europeans leaving, Karim thought of Didier. *Surely he had ceased to work at the lycée by now?* Karim wondered. *Was he still in Algeria for that matter? Perhaps he had already left?*

Karim sought to check in on Didier, despite knowing full well that the effort could be in vain. He headed over to the Lycée Bugeaud. Entering the campus, it looked rather deserted; no students nor staff in sight, so he decided to go straight to the principal's office, seeking answers. Along the way, the secretary was nowhere to be seen either. Karim continued, and the door to the principal's office was wide open. Taking a look inside, Karim spotted the principal, Monsieur Renaud, bald atop his head with short white hairs on the side, full goatee, wearing his usual bowtie and gray flannel blazer coat. He apparently was on his way out the door. A briefcase under his left armpit, a stack of papers in his right hand, he looked to be in a rush.

"What are you doing here?" Monsieur Renaud asked, rude.

"I came to see Professor Didier. I'd like to–"

Karim was cut off. "He's not here."

"Oh," Karim replied. "Well can you tell me if he–"

"Don't expect to see me here again!"

Karim was curious to dig a little deeper. "Care to clarify?"

"Have you been living under a rock? The school is shut down. Closed!" An insulting remark, Monsieur Renaud then shut the door.

"Well, if you recognized me, you would know that I dropped out of school."

"And I don't care to know." A key ring holding several keys was dangling from the man's fingers of his left hand.

As he reached for it with his right hand, he fumbled the key ring and dropped it, which only agitated him even more. "Now look what you made me do," the principal said, bending down to pick up the key ring off the floor. "The school is shut down," he repeated. "It is no longer in operation. It will be renamed to some shit Arab name. Take that to the bank." He locked his office.

"That's totally uncalled for, monsieur. Unnecessary," Karim replied.

"Everything has gone to hell in a handbasket. If there's any consolation, I'll receive a much higher salary in Europe, and I'll be spared from having to oversee the likes of you."

"Your bigotry is shining brightly."

"Oh, and don't steal any property. There's plenty of that going on around town already."

"And if I do? What will you do, notify the *gendarmes*?"

"*Foutez le camp!*" the principal yelled, upset. *Get the hell out of here!* He then stormed out of the building and left.

With no one in sight, Karim went to take a stroll down the corridor and to the classroom where the professor presided. The only audible sound was his footsteps. He could hear a pin drop; the campus was that empty, void of activity. Arriving at the classroom door, it was closed. Karim wondered at first if it might have been locked, but after reaching for the doorknob, he succeeded in turning it and opening the door. Inside, the classroom was just as he last remembered it–the position of the students' desks, the professor's desk and all else, with one exception. What *did* stand out as something out of the ordinary was the inscription on the chalkboard. Karim moved closer to the chalkboard, and focused his eyes on the writing, which said it all, in big letters: "*LE COURS EST FINI!*" Class is over.

Succinct and to the point. Karim moved away from the chalkboard and briefly looked out the window. A still courtyard. He would have liked to have said goodbye to professor Didier; at least one last meeting with him, and *that* opportunity had long passed, Karim told himself. "Why did I wait this long? I should have come by sometime ago," he muttered to himself. *Too little, too late.*

On a partly cloudy Sunday afternoon, Karim was set to catch up with Noureddine at an address close to the Cathédrale du Sacré-Coeur. Now that he was back to receiving a source of income, albeit a temporary one, courtesy of Sofiane, Karim picked up a rental car once again, taking a route which led him through the Tunnel des Facultés and onto Boulevard Saint-Saëns. There had been a recent fatal attack on an Algerian in the tunnel, and it came as no surprise that the victim was a university faculty member, given that Algiers University was situated adjacent to the tunnel. For some time, the tunnel was a checkpoint hot spot, one that the police often demanded to "see your papers," depending on one's ethnic makeup, among other things. One had to give a damn good explanation to pass through the tunnel. Ah, *"papers, please"*–a deplorable phrase reminding one of a bloody era some twenty years earlier. But, by all appearances, the checkpoint at the tunnel was now a thing of the past, as a result of the Évian Accords.

Rue Edith Cavell was mainly residential, with the upper part of the street more narrow. The meeting place was a parking lot, which, as Karim drove by it, looked to be abandoned. It led him to believe that Noureddine had scoped out this spot. Karim opted to simply park the car on the street, followed by making a short uphill walk to the lot. He looked around and found Noureddine, all the way in the back of the lot, by the wall. Noureddine stood tall, confident, feeling like a million bucks, as one would say. He approached Karim with a handshake.

"Looking good, my friend. You seem to be doing well," Karim said.

"Better than I have in quite some time. I'm busy working long days, so the money's rolling in. Soon I'll be out of my filth of a place, and into a much better place of my own. Soon, God willing," he replied.

"Not yet though. Don't act too soon. Wait until the Europeans have all, or should I say, on a mass scale, packed their bags and are gone for good, and then apartments will be available for lease for much cheaper than current prices. Surely not for pennies on the dollar. Hey, we can all dream, right? But cheaper. Just save your money, Noureddine."

"It dawned on me, what about temporarily staying in an unoccupied apartment? One vacated by Europeans, which I know would be much better than my current living conditions. What do you think?"

"I don't think it's safe at this point. There's still plenty of OAS members, and just Europeans in general, on the prowl. Wait until they have self-deported on a mass scale. It's been happening, and continues to, but their presence is still seen and felt."

Noureddine let out a gentle sigh. "Yeah. Can't disagree with that."

"Let me clarify in this manner: *If* you decide to do so anyway, you're doing so at your own risk."

"*Entendu.* Say, of the many who've already left, in an abrupt manner we can say, that means that there are likely tangible possessions and such still inside their former apartments."

A question mark at the end of that statement, Karim sensed. "I'm under the impression that you're right...yeah, probably right."

"What are the odds that bulk items in these apartments have been or will be shipped out of Algeria?"

"Bulk items?" Karim shrugged and added, "Slim to none would be my guess."

"So it has me thinking, why don't we scope out some of these unoccupied apartment units and seize any tangible property we can get our hands on?"

Karim shrugged again. "Sure. What time of day do you have in mind?"

"Oh, nighttime is preferred, without question," Noureddine answered.

"Then we ought to wait until the curfew is lifted first."

"And who knows when that will be?"

"I can't say for a fact, but I have this hunch that the curfew will be lifted fairly soon."

Noureddine nodded his head, "OK then."

"And at this time, do not even consider scoping out Bab-el-Oued. Rule it out for the time being."

"I don't know that neighborhood well at all."

"Of course not, since you're still fairly new to the city. I myself wouldn't want to be inside an apartment building in that neighborhood at this present time, for my own safety, and I've done some pretty daring stuff before."

"Point well taken. It will have to be some other neighborhood in town."

"It's kind of ironic though, I stopped by the *lycée* recently and the principal warned me not to steal any property from the school campus." Karim then shook his head, "Man, he acted like a completely rude, mean-spirited asshole towards me," he added.

"Sounds to me like he planted a seed in your head."

"Huh? What would I do by taking a piece of chalk, or some student's dirty desk?" Karim asked. "Well, on the contrary, come to think of it, some stationery would serve some use."

"What I mean is, the principal seems to have a good sense of foresight as to what's to come, but don't do any stealing of stuff from a school campus, but rather, what I'm suggesting to you."

"Clear. It's understood."

"But overall, in the grand scheme of things, is this something you really have an interest in doing?"

"I'm down with it. And I've done it before, breaking into a farmhouse and seizing bags of grains and other food."

"But in short, let's be patient, is what you're saying?"

"Exactly. Don't think that by not acting right away, it will be a missed opportunity. As more and more Europeans depart Algeria, there won't be a shortage of goods to get our hands on."

"Good point. Right you are. And you have a car, which will make the perfect getaway."

"You can forget about getting furniture in the car."

"So then, anything else that will fit in the car."

"Anything."

June 20. The curfew was finally lifted, yet the violence at the hands of the OAS did not let up. In fact, in the weeks and even days prior, schools, libraries, hospitals and other buildings had been burned down, not least of all the destruction of the Hôtel de Ville, blown up. There was nothing left for the OAS to fight for–the independence referendum only days away–and even they knew there was no chance the majority of French citizens would vote 'no' on it. What the OAS *did* find useful was to stick it to Algerians by causing mayhem and destruction of property that they believed would inevitably be claimed by Algerians.

The following day, in the evening, Karim joined Djamila at a friend's place in the neighborhood of Clos Salembier for a festive, celebratory dinner. *Chorba frik*, a green wheat soup with tomatoes and lamb meat, followed by *qalb el louz* for dessert, made of semolina, almonds and honey. Upon departure, he escorted Djamila back home, a reassurance of safety from the random assault or spurt of violence on the street.

Right after, Karim headed straight to Telemly as planned at half-past nine o'clock at night to see Noureddine, who was waiting in front of his place, idling by the street curb. "I'd feel like a coward had I not kept my word and not joined in with you on this, so here I am," Karim said.

"Glad to hear that. Let's see at least what we can find. I could have already done so on my own, but two is better than one. Much better to have another man, a friend, at my side in case something bad happens."

"Understood. Well, let's not waste any more time and get going."

They got in the car and Karim drove off promptly, with Noureddine mentioning he already had the place in mind he wanted to scope out: an apartment building in close proximity to the headquarters of the EGA, *Électricité et gaz d'Algérie*, a gasoline and electricity company. Karim drove on and arrived in little time. "You lead the way," he said to Noureddine before they got out of the car and headed to the front of the building. Noureddine gently opened the wrought iron door and then came to the staircase of the apartment. He emphasized the importance of keeping quiet, making as little noise as possible.

The two of them ascended to the third floor, which was almost pitch black throughout the corridor, save for the patch of light seen underneath one door that emanated from a nightlight. They trod softly down the corridor until they arrived at the second to last door to their right, where Noureddine noticed it wasn't closed completely. He turned to Karim, as if seeking his approval to enter. Karim locked eyes with him and gave a single nod of the head, a non-verbal *'yes, do it.'* Reaching for the doorknob, Noureddine gently turned it clockwise and proceeded to open the door, and, with the flashlight in hand and turned on, took one step in and shined the light inside. The door was then fully opened and he took another step, and another, with Karim right behind him. By all appearances, the unit was unoccupied.

Karim gently closed the door, and both men commenced to search around. The French door to the balcony was locked from the inside. Among the contents in the apartment: an antique desk, a dining table in which crumbs of food were visible–an indication that the occupants had only recently vacated the apartment–, a plush violet sofa and a *fauteuil*.

Karim searched the desk while Noureddine combed through the kitchen. The desk featured only two drawers and both were empty. Karim then moved to the bedroom, which looked extravagant compared to his standards. The large drawer chest yielded nothing except used clothing that was of no value to him. Likewise, used toiletries in the bathroom that were inutile. Moving over to the nightstand,

Karim opened the top drawer and came upon a mini treasure of a discovery–several pieces of women's jewelry: a gold necklace, an emerald necklace, a pearl bracelet, among other articles of jewelry. *Why would someone leave all this jewelry behind?* he wondered. Karim grabbed it all in one swoop of the hand.

He walked out of the bedroom and approached Noureddine, who apparently was finished with searching the kitchen. "This place is loaded with kitchenware: copper bowls, top-notch porcelain tureens, pots, pans, plates, silverware, ladles and more," Noureddine said, in a low tone.

"Wow, you've hit the cookware jackpot. We obviously can't take them all without a proper bag or container to haul them in, so we'll just come back another time when we're better prepared to carry them all?" Karim asked.

"We have to. We don't have a choice. What have you got?"

Karim stretched out his right hand. "Jewelry."

A look of amazement on Noureddine's face. "Oh my, wow! Let's not take a chance with leaving this here."

"Oh no, we're taking this with us now," Karim said, above a whisper.

"Good. I think we ought to head out now."

Noureddine flicked off the flashlight and both men quietly exited the unit, making sure the door was completely closed. Down the corridor and to the staircase, Noureddine was first to begin the descent when a man came to the bottom of the staircase. The man, appearing to be in his forties or fifties, wore a beige shirt, gray slacks and had strands of gray hair among otherwise brown hair that was slicked back, said nothing, waiting for both men to descend the staircase. Right away, Karim moved his left hand, the one clutching the jewelry, behind his back so that the man downstairs would not see the loot, if he hadn't already. As soon as Karim made it to the bottom of the staircase, the man moved towards him and reached for his arm, saying, "What have you here? Is this–"

Immediately, Noureddine encroached, putting both hands on the man and then pushing him against the wall, to which he was met with some resistance by the stranger. "Just mind your own business, sir, and move along," Noureddine said.

The stranger resisted, bringing his hands up, close to Noureddine's neck, saying nothing. Noureddine tightened his grip on him and said, "I don't want to hit you. Don't force me to."

To no avail, the man refused to heed the warning, tussling with Noureddine. Within seconds, Noureddine managed to club him across the face with a right fist, causing him to fall on the floor, shaken. Karim said to Noureddine, "Let's go! Let's get out of here!"

They both stormed through the wrought iron door, out of the apartment building and into the car. Karim handed the jewelry over to Noureddine, who put it on his lap, and drove off. "Good thing we got out of there right away. Hopefully another tenant didn't catch that incident there," Karim said.

"Let's hope not. Had I not been present with you, no doubt it would have resulted in a full-fledged fight between you and that man."

"And that right there could have been serious, if not deadly."

"Perhaps it might not be a good idea to return, after that encounter. We couldn't manage to make it out of there unseen."

"Well, at least we tried."

"But you made out with *this*," Noureddine said, referencing the jewelry.

"It's something."

"Here, you hold onto the jewelry. After all, you discovered it."

Karim was a bit frantic in his driving, and in an agitated reaction, responded, "Just put it in the glove compartment. I'll figure it out later." Noureddine did so without question. In no time, the car pulled up in front of his residence. Noureddine got of the car, grateful for Karim. "Thanks for all you've done and for joining me tonight, in spite of that scuffle that took place. You're someone I can count on."

"As always. But I am the one indebted to you now for coming to my aid," Karim said. "Good night."

Karim had a hard time getting a good night's sleep, attributing it to the burglary and the subsequent scuffle. A disturbing dream conjured up a scene inside the same apartment building where he was caught in the act of stealing by a tenant and then brutally attacked, inside the very same unit he and Noureddine had entered. *This time*, Karim was in a fierce struggle for his life as the physical altercation had escalated. It all came to an end when he suddenly woke up around eight o'clock in the morning, realizing it was merely a dream.

He decided to stop by Sebastián's office, as Karim hadn't seen nor heard from Sebastián in a few weeks at least. Karim's siblings were occupied with playing a board game in the living room when he walked out the door, on his way to the car. Before driving off, he retrieved an unloaded revolver and several bullets from the trunk, tucking them in the pocket of his cardigan as a protective measure in entering and moving about Bab-el-Oued. Two 10-franc notes that were given to him the day before by Noureddine came in handy to put fuel in the car.

The scene at the roundabout of the Place des Trois Horloges was bustling, and even chaotic at times. Residents seemingly on their way out, in a rush, carrying suitcases, the honking of car horns and shouts of anger. Karim parked directly in front of the law office in knowing that the tramway was not in operation, and made a quick entry into the building. Ascending the stairwell to the second floor, he soon found the door to the office was unlocked, allowing him to enter easily. Karim moved around without haste. Mathilde was nowhere to be seen. As it turned out, the office was unoccupied and abandoned. Yet, the office furniture remained, stationery neatly organized and not scattered about the desk. The window was concealed by a large white curtain. In opening the drawers of the filing cabinets, all documents, all paperwork had been cleared out. Empty file folders were all that remained.

Karim entered Sebastián's office. He was nowhere to be seen either. The framed photographs of various Spanish cities still hung on the walls, however, the plaques and framed images that featured Sebastián's name or mugshot were gone. In seeking any sort of answers, Karim went ahead and searched the office, starting with the desk and its drawers. Some handwritten scribble on a notepad looked to be irrelevant, yielding no hints nor clues. He moved aside the executive chair and then opened the top of the desk's three drawers on the right. Postage-paid envelopes that bore the law office's address as the sender on the top left, its contents empty inside. In the middle drawer, yellow copies of bank deposit slips in which the numbers written were barely legible. Nothing out of the ordinary.

He then opened the bottom drawer, and to his surprise, came upon a sealed envelope, one that was simply addressed to "KARIM," in big, ALL CAPS letters, handwritten. Karim reached for a letter opener on the desk and slid it through the envelope's flap, taking hold of a letter inside, handwritten on beige stationery paper.

> *Dear Karim,*
>
> *Due to unforeseen circumstances, my wife and I had to abruptly leave Algeria, for good. Please accept my sincere apologies for not being able to say goodbye to you in person. As I'm sure you're fully aware of, the Post Office is not in operation and I'm hoping this letter gets to you by way of you stopping by my office. In hindsight, we should have fled much sooner and not make our departure well into June. In any case, I hope you're doing well and staying safe and sound. It has been a great pleasure in being acquainted with you, and working with you as well. On the back of this letter, you'll find my residential address in Spain, where you can send me correspondence, as well as my phone number, should you feel you'd like to chat.*
>
> *P.S. – Feel free to take anything from my office as you see fit, before someone else does.*
>
> *Sincerely,*
>
> *Sebastián Ruiz*

Karim turned the letter to the back, and, as stated, it revealed an address in Alicante, and a phone number. Well, at least it wouldn't be the last he'd ever hear from Sebastián again, and that was good news to Karim.

July 5. The GPRA proclaimed "July 5" to be Algeria's Independence Day, following de Gaulle signing an agreement, officially recognizing Algeria as an independent, sovereign state just two days prior. Karim was eager to descend onto the streets that were bound to be boisterous; an explosion of Algerian joy. He left home at a quarter to noon and in approaching the Moorish café in the Lower Casbah, he saw several people outside the café, mingling and socializing. *Are they waiting to get in?* Karim wondered. He drew closer and recognized a few of them as neighbors. "Hey, what's going on?" he asked.

"We're celebrating!" replied one of the neighbors, Ismail, a cheery grin gracing his face, a man who was employed as a locksmith. "Head right in. Grab a drink."

Karim entered the café and it was a full house, to his delight. Lively, full of chatter and elation, he'd never seen this café anywhere near this packed. He could not help but to give a huge smile, knowing full well that the goal was now realized. Mission accomplished! Karim wedged himself between several patrons in making his way to the counter. Ali, the owner, in his late fifties, had combed back gray hair and cocoa-colored skin, stood beside the counter and was quick to greet Karim.

"Karim, my friend," Ali said, receiving him with a warm hug, Karim reciprocating. "Independence is here! We're free from the colonizer at last."

"Ah, man, the victory we've all been longing for!" Karim replied, letting out an exclamation of relief and joy. "Whew! I can't begin to tell you the struggle, the relentless effort we've all put in to make this come to fruition."

"What had been a land that did not belong to us; a land seized by an invader. Well, we can now put that to rest. Let me get you a coffee," Ali said. In no time, he had one of his employees prepare a strong, thick black coffee, served in a copper mug. Karim turned around and took in the energetic ambiance of the café, amazed by it. A celebration unlike any he had ever experienced. Ali brought the coffee to Karim. "Indulge in it!"

Karim took one sip, and another. Sweet and frothy, just the way he liked his coffee. "Splendid, I love it."

"It doesn't get any better than this," Ali said, observing the patrons and basking in the atmosphere.

"I'm going to check out the scene on the streets." Karim finished the last of the coffee before heading out the door.

Departing the Casbah, Karim proceeded on foot. The scorching heat beamed down on the city. It had to be at least 100-degree weather. The scene on the streets resembled a raucous procession, one enormous in size. Cars were unable to pass by on some streets as the pedestrians took over. Chants of liberty and freedom from Algerians persisted, amidst Europeans also passing through the streets in seeking passage out of Algiers, nearly all of whom were carrying suitcases and other personal belongings, with children being held closely to their side. Karim made it to Rue d'Isly, and just ahead, a rather telling scene was unfolding. A mini specialty *épicerie* was being looted by, from all appearances, Algerians. One person after another entered and then exited the small grocery store, carrying canned goods, bags of pasta and whatever other food products they could get their hands on. Karim approached to get an up-close view, but had no interest whatsoever in joining the looters. Another European business being looted by the victims of colonization.

As Karim carried on, drawing closer to the Aletti Hotel, a sea of red, white and green emerged, exalting in jubilation that for the people of Algeria, their time had come. Civilians joined ALN soldiers in ascending and then standing on the beds of military cargo trucks, waving Algerian flags as the vehicles drove leisurely through the streets of town. Karim arrived within feet of the city's Joan of Arc statue, which a passerby had draped with an Algerian flag. La Grande Poste d'Alger was only a stone's throw away. He wiped sweat off his forehead with the upper sleeve of his shirt, and then turned to face the bay. Many Europeans were passing by on foot, their hands full with carrying suitcases. Children, clutching onto precious dolls, uncomprehending of the situation at hand. One girl, perhaps no more than five years old, was crying profusely, tears running down her cheeks, as if she knew right then, even at her age, that she would probably not see Algeria again—at least not any-time soon. The woman holding onto the little girl's hand, presumably the mother, pulled her closer and squeezed her hand, making sure she could not escape. Karim, watching this, was slowly overtaken with emotions; seeing a mother and father with their distressed child. Suddenly, he was struck with a flashback of his father, who was physically beaten to death in an ambush in front of Karim's own eyes. A father absent in his life. "Papa," Karim whispered to himself. "Papa, I miss you so much."

Out of nowhere, a hand was placed on Karim's shoulder from behind, startling him, causing him to nearly jump. In turning around, he also took a step back. "Karim," the man said. It took a few seconds for Karim to come to the realization that it was Professor Didier!

"My God, you scared me," Karim admitted.

"I'm sorry. What a pleasant surprise to see you. How have you been? I haven't seen you in ages, it seems." Didier was clutching onto a large suitcase and accompanied by a woman, whom Karim presumed to be his wife, also carrying one as well.

"I'm doing all right, Professor. I've just been…how can I say it, I've been playing an active role throughout this whole…*conflict*, I guess you can call it."

Didier nodded his head. "Yes, as I last recall. By the way, this is my wife, Séverine."

"Hello, madame," Karim said.

Séverine gave a sort of shy response of "Hello," accompanied by a soft smile.

Karim turned back to Didier and said, "I'm glad you're safe and sound, Professor. I stopped by the school in May and was told that you were no longer there due to the closure. I wondered if you had already left Algeria, or God forbid, you got caught in the crosshairs of all the violence and might have met a fatal encounter."

"Oh no, I've made it through all of this, thank God," Didier replied.

"I'm sorry. I should have stopped by campus to see you a long time ago, and I regret it. No excuse for it."

"No worries. No harm done." Didier then let out a sigh. "Well, this is it, my friend. The end of colonial rule."

"It's now a reality."

"The ship we're to catch is up ahead. We're headed to Marseille. We'll be staying with family for the time being until we get ourselves better situated. Karim, please do come and pay us a visit in Marseille in the future, when you see fit. My invitation to you."

"I promise. You have my word, I'll pay you a visit in France someday." Karim pulled out a pen and a piece of paper from his front pocket. He wrote down a phone number of one of Didier's relatives living in France, whom

Karim could call as a means of getting ahold of Didier in the future.

"I'm proud to have called you a student of mine. Take care and I wish you the best." Didier set his suitcase down on the ground momentarily and went in and gave Karim a hug. Karim was grateful to have known such a man.

"Thank you. Please stay safe out there. Things can get out of hand and crazy."

"Will do."

"Isn't it something, that we're standing feet away from the Joan of Arc statue. Talk about a hero to the French."

Didier seemed to think hard about how he wanted to respond. "Indeed." He continued, "But you know what? Algeria needs a hero of its own." He looked away for a moment, gave a nod of the head, and then met Karim's eyes. "Yeah, a hero."

It took a moment or so for Karim to fully grasp the message that was truly being conveyed to him. He gave a soft grin. "Yes, I see what you mean."